Unravel

SHARON JENNINGS

Red Deer Press

Published in Canada by Red Deer Press, 195 Allstate Parkway, Markham, ON L3R 4T8

Published in the United States by Red Deer Press, 311 Washington Street, Brighton, MA 02135

Red Deer Press acknowledges with thanks the Canada Council for the Arts and the Ontario Arts Council for their support of our publishing program. We acknowledge the financial support of the Government of Canada through the Canada Book Fund (CBF) for our publishing activities.

Library and Archives Canada Cataloguing in Publication
Title: Unravel / Sharon Jennings.
Names: Jennings, Sharon, 1954- author.
Identifiers: Canadiana 20200362119 | ISBN 9780889956193 (softcover)
Classification: LCC PS8569.E563 U57 2021 | DDC jC813/.54—dc23

Publisher Cataloging-in-Publication Data (U.S.)
Names: Jennings, Sharon, 1954-, author.
Title: Unravel / Sharon Jennings.
Description: Markham, Ontario : Red Deer Press, 2021. | Summary: "As Rebecca is about to turn twelve years old, she begins to realize that Joe, her father, seems to want to turn her away from anyone who might intrude on their two lives. Life changes for Rebecca the day that she spots a new neighbor, Phoebe, a woman who has an aura of elegance about her and who also takes an immediate interest in the girl. As Rebecca gets to know Phoebe better, she also is able to look at Joe with different eyes and she realizes that her father is not at all who he has presented himself to be" -- Provided by publisher.
Identifiers: ISBN 978-0-88995-619-3 (paperback)
Subjects: LCSH: Parent and child -- Juvenile fiction. | Emotional maturity -- Juvenile fiction. | Intergenerational relations -- Juvenile fiction. | BISAC: YOUNG ADULT FICTION / Family / General.
Classification: LCC PZ7.J466Unr | DDC 813.6 – dc23

Edited for the Press by Peter Carver
Text and cover design by Tanya Montini
Printed in Canada by Houghton Boston

www.reddeerpress.com

To Allison Blum,
who is always eager to be my first reader.

And to my late mother-in-law, Maria DiLena,
the inspiration for Mrs. Martino.

Why I Am Writing

There were plenty of signs my life didn't make sense, and I guess adults should have paid more attention. They noticed when I had dirty fingernails or egg yolk on my sweatshirt, and they always asked why I wasn't in school. Joe said to tell any nosy parker I was homeschooled. If they asked too often, well ... Joe said it was time to move.

I am writing this because Phoebe said I should. Phoebe is a partial recluse and my friend. A recluse, in case you don't know, is someone who doesn't want to be bothered with the world and people asking questions, and so goes into seclusion (which is a sort of hiding). I think it usually only applies to someone famous. Phoebe didn't want to be alone all the time, but she said she liked to keep a low profile. Phoebe's full name is Phoebe St. Claire and she has a movie star name, which, cross my heart, I've vowed never to reveal.

Phoebe said writing about what happened to me would help. She even said it would be fun! "And it'll show all the silly people that you're *not* messed up." Phoebe said that because my first therapist said I was damaged, like I was a car in an accident.

The White King in *Alice in Wonderland* said if you want to write a good story, you begin at the beginning, go on to the end, and then stop. This poses a predicament. I didn't know my beginning for a long time. So I'm going to begin with the day, the awful day, that was really the beginning of the end.

The Day That Was
The Beginning of the End

He took me to a book festival for my twelfth birthday. September 26th, 2004. We used to go to lots of book things for adults, like readings and author signings in stores. This one was outside at a pioneer village, with folding chairs set out in groups, all along the Main Street, so people could sit and hear famous writers read their work. And this time it was mostly authors who wrote for kids.

We sat at the back at each reading. I wanted to move up close because sometimes the writers didn't have microphones.

"If I can't hear them, what's the point?"

"Sitting at the back is fine."

"But ..."

"I said ..." Joe didn't finish his sentence. Just expected me to agree, as I almost always did. I folded my arms across my chest and slumped in my seat.

Before the reading began, someone said something like this. "Hey, folks. Let's make like pioneers and turn off our cell phones." They also said a newspaper photographer was hanging about, and I wanted to ask if the pioneers minded cameras, but I knew it would be rude.

I hoped the photographer would take my picture. If it got in the paper, maybe all the people I've met would see it and remember me. And I did want to be famous one day. Maybe this would be the start.

I listened to the authors and watched for the photographer. At one reading, he was moving toward the back rows, snapping constantly, and then Joe said he saw a better seat and hustled me so far away, we were practically sitting in the back row of another reading, listening to another author!

Near the end of the day, he wanted to hear an adult book author. I did NOT want to listen to an adult writer. Joe had read lots of adult books to me ever since I could remember. He let me interrupt him and ask questions when I didn't know a word or when I could not figure out what on earth the author was talking about. Once he read a play called *Waiting for Godot*. It's got only four characters in it, and Joe did all the voices so I'd know who was talking.

I'm glad he did because the play is hard to understand. He said it's about how bleak and dreary life is for some people.

"Well, of course life is bleak and dreary!" I pointed out. "These two tramps just wait around on an empty road for some guy to show up. And he doesn't. Show up, I mean."

After that he read another play called *Death of a Salesman*, and I became heartily sick of adults being bleak and dreary. Then came *The Importance of Being Earnest*, which sounded like another serious problem, but it turned out to be very silly.

Anyway, I absolutely refused to listen to this adult author and began my campaign. "Jean Little's over there. You know I love her books. There is no logical reason why you can't stay here and I go listen to her."

"Keep away from that photographer. You hear me?"

"Why? What's the big deal?"

"I don't want a photo of you in a paper," he answered. "You know that."

"That was before. That was when you were worried about Mother's family. But you said it didn't matter anymore. You said we're safe."

"Do you want to go home? Right now? Do you?"

"No."

He watched me until I took my seat in the back row, out in front of Ye Olde One Room Schoolhouse.

Soon other people blocked me from his view and, when he turned away, I jumped up and changed seats so that I was in the front row and could almost pat Jean Little's Seeing Eye dog. (An aside: everybody knows you're not supposed to pat someone's Seeing Eye dog!)

I soon figured out how this gig worked. If I asked the author a bunch of questions and acted precocious, the photographer would notice me.

And that's what happened. I said things like, "I really love your books," and "How long does it take you to write a book?" and "I want to write books when I grow up." (I didn't, particularly, but authors like to hear this stuff.) And I told her what my favorite book was. I heard the click, click, click of the camera, and I tossed my hair off my face and smiled, all the while my heart pounding with the thrill of it and the fear of what I was doing.

"Your folks okay with me taking a couple of shots?" the photographer asked.

"Not a problem," I lied, digging my fingernails into my palms.

"You sure are a big fan. Can I have your name?"

"Rebecca. Rebecca Greene. Greene with an 'e'."

"And why are you here today, Rebecca Greene with an 'e'?"

My cue. "Books are my life! I devour books. I read all day and pretend I know the people in the books, and make up more adventures for them, with me in them, too." I added the cherry on top. "And it's my birthday today."

He wrote it all down and smiled. "Happy birthday."

"Are you sure I'll be in the paper?"

"*The Village Times*. Next Thursday. I'll make sure you get in—a pretty girl like you."

I blushed. I wasn't pretty, even though Phoebe said I was. Joe doesn't believe in that stuff, calling attention to yourself with trendy clothes or fashionable haircuts. If forced to describe my appearance, I would have to honestly say I was a cross between a beanbag chair and a sheepdog.

I looked up and saw Joe staring, and my tummy clenched. He put down the book he was buying and almost flew across the clearing. I ran and watched from behind Ye Olde Port-a-Potty. He grabbed the photographer's arm and the photographer stiffened. But he showed his camera and Joe peered into the screen, and then I saw the photographer do something and I knew. I knew he was erasing the photos of me.

Joe marched over. "Let's go." He didn't yell. He smiled. The bad smile. A lady stepping out of the toilet stopped to stare. And the bad smile and the bad smell got stuck together and are part of that awful day.

"What are you looking at?" he snapped. The lady frowned, but she didn't say anything.

He took my arm and tried to drag me along, but I dug my heels into the dirt. "That's enough. You're making a scene. Because you can't behave in public, we're going home." Then he pinched.

"OUCH!"

He let go of my arm and looked around. Something swelled up inside that I couldn't control. Like a ball you try to hold underwater until you can't.

"I don't want to go home. It's my birthday!"

"You should have thought of that before acting up."

Acting up? I wasn't three years old. And I wasn't acting up, anyway. I stuck out my tongue when he turned his back.

This day had started out so well, considering all the fights over the last month. When he said he wanted to make amends, and wanted to take me to buy books, brand new books for my birthday, I had almost dared to hope things might be improving. I knew there was nothing to say to make him change his mind about leaving the festival. But I wanted some answers. I was twelve, and too many things weren't making sense.

I was wearing a sweater I got at Goodwill the day before, a present I bought myself so I would have something new on my birthday. I noticed the sleeve had a loose bit of yarn and I picked at it on the bus ride home. Pretty soon, I realized, I could unravel the whole thing.

Joe reached over and slapped my hand. "Stop that," he said.

Why I Have No Mother

I don't want to write about the rest of that awful day just yet. So, I think I'll go back a bit and tell something about my life. Sometimes things get remembered in no particular order and I write them down. Phoebe says it'll all get straightened out somehow. She says, "Just put pieces together when you can. Like when you're doing a jigsaw puzzle. You know how you figure out that all the yellow must be the sun in the top right corner? And all the green is the grass along the bottom edge?"

Here goes.

As far back as I could remember, I lived with Joe. Just the two of us. My mom died when I was born. It was my fault, Joe said, because I was a very big baby and it hurt her.

Joe told me all this when I was little, maybe six. About my mom, I mean. He said her name was Diana, and I liked that because it's the name of a Greek goddess. Growing up, that's how I thought of my mom—a goddess, too good for this earth. And even though I never met her, sometimes I had dreams about her when I was really little, before I was six and Joe told me. I'd wake up crying, "Mommy! Mommy!" And I was scared.

Her death happened so fast, Joe said there was no time for photos of me and her. So, I didn't have even one picture of me and my mom. Some kids have pictures of their moms holding them right after birth. You can see the hospital room and the doctor and nurses and all the equipment. Or the bedroom if it was a homebirth. My friend Jordan has a picture of herself in a pink blanket, and her mom's holding her in one arm and using the other hand to phone someone. Jordan has three brothers, so her mom was really excited when she finally got a girl. Sebastian is the brother born two years before Jordan. He always teased me and was a real pain.

But what I couldn't figure out was why we didn't have any pictures of my mom at all. No photos of my parents dating and not even one on the day of their wedding. It occurred to me to ask about this when I was a little older. Nine, I think.

He said it was because he went berserk when she died.

"I was just so crazy with grief, Rebby, that I destroyed every photo of her. I was so angry at her for dying on us that I went nuts and ripped up every picture and threw out all her things. I know it doesn't make sense, but grief does that to some people. Do you understand?"

Well, no, I certainly did not. But Joe was giving me his sad puppy look, so I nodded and tried to look sympathetic. It was my fault she died, after all. I even hugged him, but I felt bleak and dreary for days. Didn't he stop to think that I might want a picture of my mom? He was selfish, was all. I barely spoke to him for a week.

Sullivan Street

We moved around a lot, usually every few months, and a couple of times after a week or two. My favorite place was the second floor of a co-op of row houses on Sullivan Street where we each had a bedroom. There was a balcony over a small garden and, because there were only two floors, I could pretend we were living in a house of our own.

We lived there for almost a year and I even had a cat named Ollie. At first Joe thought it was great because, when he was working, the other tenants looked out for me. But one summer day I overheard Mrs. Martino talking to him in her kitchen. I was supposed to be picking caterpillars off the arugula, but when I heard my name, well, of course, I tiptoed to the window and listened. (Not for nothing had I read *Harriet the Spy*.)

"It's not right, Joe," Mrs. Martino said. "Rebecca shouldn't be home all day alone. She's eleven years old.

She needs to be in school, making friends." She said all that with a heavy Italian accent, but I don't want to write it that way in case someone thinks I'm making fun of her.

"She's fine, Mrs. Martino. Rebecca is a very happy little girl."

Well, that was true. But why did Mrs. Martino think I should go to school? I thought she liked having me around all day. And as for school, I know lots of kids go, but so what? Joe believed in homeschooling and, so far, it was working just fine, thank you very much.

"Of course she is happy. She reads all day long and talks to everyone in the neighborhood, and we teach her things and give her good things to eat. But," Mrs. Martino lowered her voice, "she's growing up wild."

Wild? Me?

Joe disagreed. "Don't exaggerate."

But I could tell Mrs. Martino was working herself up to be emotional. "Joe, Joe! Look at her. Use your eyes. She looks like a boy, all big baggy clothes. And that hair! No shape. No style. How can she grow up to be a woman?"

Joe, suddenly very loud and clear, said, "Time enough for that, Mrs. Martino. No need to rush a female into puberty."

But Mrs. Martino wasn't done, just because Joe was using his I'm finished arguing voice.

"Ha! You men. So stupeeed." (There—I did her accent thing.) "Puberty comes when it comes, bello. No father can stop it. And then—look out! I'ma warning you. Sheeza no a leettle girl anymore. Capisce?"

"Do you capisce that it is none of your business?" Uh-oh. That was his bad voice.

Mrs. Martino said something in Italian. I'm pretty sure it was swearing. At least I hoped so.

I heard a chair squeak on the old wooden floor, and I hustled on my knees to the closer patch of radicchio.

I was supposed to kill the caterpillars but I didn't. I usually dropped them over the fence into Mr. Popolopolos's yard. But when Mrs. Martino called me wild, I felt a kinship with the caterpillar tickling my palm and snuck it into my bedroom. I placed it in a cut-glass marmalade jar and put in a stick and grass and punched holes in the lid. Maybe if it turned into a beautiful butterfly, it would be an omen that I would turn into a beautiful woman. Because, after I heard Mrs. Martino talk about me becoming a woman, I was kind of intrigued by the idea. It had never occurred to me that in the future

I might look like Mrs. Martino, all big bosoms and full derriere (French for bum) and comfy tummy. One day, Joe referred to her as fat.

"She shouldn't dress like that."

"Like what?" I asked.

"Those tight skirts she wears and those tight V-neck sweaters. She's too old and too fat."

"Mr. Martino doesn't mind."

Joe said, "If I were Mr. Martino, I'd soon straighten her out."

But I knew Joe was wrong. Mr. Martino was always putting his arms around her and squeezing, and once I saw him pinch her derriere. She laughed and smacked his hand away, but then she pulled him into her body and gave him an enormous kiss, and they smiled at each other as if they were two kids with a big secret.

Joe never let me wear tight clothes. One day we went to Goodwill and I saw a pair of totally unworn jeans. I tried them on and they fit! I've used an exclamation mark on purpose because the clothes Joe bought me were always baggy.

When I showed Joe, he scowled and said, "Take them off!"

I argued and cajoled (that is just a fancy word for arguing with a bit of puppy-dog eyes thrown in). "But I won't need a belt! And they're brand new. This is a great deal, Joe."

"Absolutely not. No daughter of mine is going around showing every inch of her body."

I kept it up for a bit and then he said, "Reb, you know I hate to pull rank, but ..." Joe never finishes this sentence, just looks disappointed in me. The end result was I went home with a pair of baggy jeans twelve sizes too big. He said, "You'll grow into them." Which is absurd, because I will wear them out in a month. (More about that anon— which is Shakespeare for later.) We went for ice cream after, which is Joe's way of saying he's sorry for pulling rank. The whole thing smacks of ~~hipokrazy~~ hypocrisy because adults enjoy pulling rank.

Where was I? Oh, yes.

After Mrs. Martino said I was growing up wild, Joe asked me if I wanted to go to school.

"Wherever did you get an idea like that?" I asked, my eyes wide open. I really was shocked because Joe always talked about school as a tool of the establishment and government interference. But there was something else going on. Like he was daring me to ... to have an idea different from his.

"Are you happy, Rebby?"

This was trickier. I knew I was supposed to say, "Yes." And I was happy, but what if I could be happier? What if there was a better way to do things and I didn't know about it? It isn't fair to ask kids these big questions when they don't know all the alternatives. I believe it's called a set-up.

"What are you suggesting?" I asked, and thought I was so clever, replying with a question.

"Nothing. Nothing at all. Just wondered if you might like to go to school one day? Like other kids." He watched me with narrowed eyes, and I was a bit scared of giving the wrong answer.

I shrugged. Of course, it might be nice to have friends my own age, all held captive in one room, and maybe wear one of those Britishy-looking uniforms. Visions of Hogwarts danced in my head! But what if I didn't want to go to school every day? What if I wanted to sleep in or spend the day drawing, or help Mrs. Martino in the garden or work at the corner store with Mr. Chung? Some mornings I walked Jordan to her school and she always fussed about being on time. So, I knew a ~~lassy-fair~~ laissez-faire approach to attendance wasn't allowed.

Still … some days I felt a bit jealous. Like when other girls yelled, "Hi" to Jordan and linked arms and they went through the door together, and I was left outside. Some days I didn't mind. But other days … well … other days it was hard to fill the hours by myself.

But … I liked the way Joe homeschooled me. Mostly, he read to me. I read all the time myself, but he read books that would be difficult, even for me. I sat on the floor at his feet and he poked me if I was falling asleep. That was pretty much it for my homeschooling with Joe. He knew I helped Mr. Chung in his store and learned about arithmetic, and about weighing things and doing the cash. And he knew Mrs. Martino taught me to cook and told me about Italy and World War Two. He probably didn't know Mrs. Martino called the leader "bastardo Mussolini." And when she said bastardo Mussolini, she always spit on the floor twice. Spit! Spit! Up until I was eleven, Joe used to do a lot more with me, but over the last year, he said he had to work harder to earn enough money.

"Do I have to decide about school right now?"

"Nope. Don't rock the boat, that's my advice."

But that didn't make sense because Joe did rock the boat. A few weeks before my twelfth birthday, he announced, "I've found us a better place to live."

No. Oh, no. Not this again. My stomach cramped.

"How can there be a better place to live than Sullivan Street?" I wailed.

He didn't answer. He didn't have to. It was because Mrs. Martino was too nosy.

The Beige

We went to see this "better place to live," all the way at the end of Queen Street, and I hated it, just like I knew I would. (An aside: I was kind of intrigued that Lake Ontario came almost up to the road, but I didn't tell Joe that.)

It was a tall building and the apartment we looked at was on the fourteenth floor—except it was really the thirteenth because people are superstitious, and so they just pretend there isn't a thirteenth floor and leave the number off the elevator panel. I think that must be what they mean when they say: Out of sight, out of mind.

We went in through a shabby beige lobby and then up the grungy elevator to the thirteenth floor, and then down a long, long beige hallway marked with scuffs and dubious stains, and finally to our door. Inside, the walls were beige, with a particularly odious gloss.

The superintendent glared at us. "The walls stay beige.

Ya hear me?" Then she scowled at me. "None of yer psycherdellic paint jobs. Ya hear?" (She really did talk like this, and so I'm writing like this because I don't care if you think I'm making fun of her.)

"Rent's due first day of the month and no loud noise. Ya got questions?"

Joe said, "None," and handed her an envelope. My jaw dropped.

"What are you doing?" I shrieked. "You said we were coming to look. You didn't tell me we were moving for sure!"

The horrid woman glared at me. "You need a smackin'." Then, to Joe, "That was my kid, I'd teach her some manners."

"If I were your child, madam," I said in my best upper-crusty British accent (and remembering to use the past subjunctive—"were" not "was"), "I would jump off the thirteenth-floor balcony!"

"That's enough, Reb. Thank you, Mrs. Heaney." He held open the front door—*our* front door. "We'll be moving in two weeks Saturday." Joe closed the door in her face even as she was gearing up to say something else.

When he turned back to me, I had my hands on my hips and was spitting angry. "How could you do this to me? I hate this place! Hate it! I won't move. I won't!"

"You haven't given this place a chance. Take a look around." He didn't raise his voice. He leaned back against the wall, his arms folded across his chest.

I stalked through the apartment. A sliver of a windowless kitchen, a dining room and a living room making an "L" shape, a windowless bathroom, one bedroom.

"There's only one bedroom."

"You get the bedroom. I'll give you money to fix it up."

"What about you?"

"I can sleep on the couch. Or I'll put a futon on the dining room floor. Whatever. I don't care."

But this meant that anytime I left my bedroom, he'd be there. He'd never be behind a closed door.

"I don't want you to sleep on the couch because of me. If we stay on Sullivan, we both have our own rooms."

Joe looked away from me. "Truth is, Reb, the neighbors are getting a little nosy for my taste. Always butting in on us and the way we live. You know I hate that."

"When?" I demanded. "When did the neighbors ever butt in on us?" Of course I knew who he meant.

"Rebecca ..." (Stern voice.)

But I was not to be persuaded quite so easily. "Give me an example. Just one example!"

"That retired teacher, Mr. Popolopolos. He said you should be in school, and he thinks it might be his duty to look into it. He was trying to threaten me and I didn't like the look on his face."

I felt sorry for Mr. Popolopolos. He was used to bossing kids around, but he didn't stand a chance against Joe. Nobody did. Joe always was so certain he knew best. If someone disagreed with him, he didn't argue. He might pretend to agree, and then continue on as before. Sometimes he simply looked through people as though they weren't there. And if I disagreed with him, he had a variety of ways to let me know.

Last winter I was reading a book I found on the subway. I could tell from the cover it was going to have some sex in it. (Or I hoped so, at any rate. This was the one thing Joe would *not* talk about.)

"That book isn't for you. Stop reading it," he said.

"Oh, but I can't! It's so good I can't put it down!"

He had this way of tilting his head and looking at me that made me think he'd never seen me before. As if I were some curious, unknown species he wanted to put under the microscope. He did it then. But he didn't take the book out of my hands.

I was reading the book in bed and fell asleep, and in the morning I looked everywhere, but couldn't find it.

"You took it, didn't you!" I accused him.

He didn't answer me. But when I went to make some tea for myself, I found my china mug, handle broken, in the kitchen sink. I didn't see the connection, of course, until it happened again and yet again when I contradicted him. A necklace cut and beads all over the floor. A new (tight) T-shirt torn.

Joe pushed himself off the beige wall and put his arm around me. "Don't be angry with me, Rebby. I want the best for us. For you. I believe kids should have some freedom. Not be trapped by the status quo. And no one is going to tell *me* how to raise my daughter."

That's why we moved the last time, too. We were in a basement, and the people who owned the house kept saying it was mighty peculiar that a girl lived with her dad and didn't go to school. That place we just left one day when the owners were out. If you don't own much stuff, it's pretty easy to walk away. Or slink away, I should say. The only good thing about leaving that basement was that we found Sullivan Street.

Standing in this awful apartment, I tried one more

time. "But I love Sullivan Street. I love our neighbors. They're ... they're like family to me."

"Well, they're not, are they?"

I knew the signs. The "discussion" was over, and I should behave.

Joe sulked, his voice as whiny as a five-year-old's. "They're not family. You and I are family. We're all the family we've got."

"What about Ollie?"

"What about him?"

"We can bring him here, right?

"He isn't our cat."

"Not our cat? But he loves me! I feed him milk every day. What will become of him?"

"Reb, he's a tomcat. He doesn't belong to anyone. He prowls about and he's found a good thing back there, but he won't notice that you're gone."

That got me. Not just about losing Ollie. But about "not notice that you're gone." Nobody ever seemed to notice when I was gone. And why should that be? We had moved around a lot, lived in lots of flats and basements and moldy apartments. And not always in this city. I remember some stuff clearly, like seeing a wheat field—

and some stuff not clearly, like a restaurant called The Big Nickel. Why? What's a big nickel? But no matter how many places, nobody ever looked us up or sent a letter or a birthday card to me or anything. Why not? I mean, I do take up space.

And there was another thing.

"Why *don't* we have any family?"

"Not this again."

"Why? Why 'not this again'? You brought it up. You said, 'We're all the family we've got.' So why can't I know why I don't have any family?"

"Look. I ..." Joe suddenly deflated and his shoulders drooped. They did. I've read that line in books but I actually saw it happen—like a blow-up doll losing some air. "Listen. Let's get something to eat. One day, I promise, I will do my best to explain."

"When?"

"Soon."

"When soon?"

He didn't answer, just gave me a new set of keys. And the fact that he already had the keys to this bleak and dreary building made me realize I had no say in my life.

The Day I Saw Phoebe

So there I was, scowling, I must admit, and dragging my feet as Joe marched through the beige lobby. He said, "Stop scuffing your shoes!" Which is ridiculous because I got them at Goodwill already scuffed. I was going to point this out to him but then ...

I saw her.

She had her key in the lock as we approached the lobby door of the building. I was a few steps away, and Joe finally told me to knock it off and hurry up. I sighed—the-world-as-we-know-it-has-come-to-an-end sigh—and this woman held the door open and smiled at me.

She had huge black sunglasses and a scarf wrapped around her head. She wore a trench coat belted tight at an impossibly tiny waist, and sky-high heels, and so much perfume that I could smell it on me all the way back to Sullivan Street. (Joe didn't let me wear perfume and called it "gunk.") Her lips were brick red and her trench coat was beige, but definitely NOT the beige of the bleak and dreary foyer. She shook out a wet umbrella with some plaid markings on it that matched her coat.

I felt an ache inside me. That's what it was—an ache. Because I'd never, ever seen anyone so perfectly perfect except in a magazine. And because I knew I could never look like her, so exquisitely polished. As if to prove me right, the door swung a bit and I saw myself reflected in the glass—a shapeless, scruffy blob. In that instant, all my dreams of a glamorous womanhood died. No one would ever look at me the way they must—had to—look at her.

She smiled at me and I fell in love. Because the smile was for me, just for me. It was an "I know how you feel, kid" smile. Our first connection as conspirators.

"Reb!"

I turned to Joe in a daze. "Huh?"

"Hurry up if you want something to eat."

But I didn't want to eat anything, then or ever. I wanted to stare at this woman. Did she live in this apartment building? How could she? She was so chic and this building was so ... so ... mundane. But if she did live here ... and, after all, she did have a key for the door. She got on the elevator and, as the door began to close, she slid her sunglasses down a bit and winked at me. At me! My heart flipped.

And as we left the building, it struck me that Joe hadn't noticed her, hadn't looked at her. How could a man not notice someone as glamorous as her?

We ran through the rain for the Queen streetcar. (Hmmm. Why was she wearing sunglasses in the rain?)

I hoped Jordan was home. I had to tell her my news, the tragic news about me moving—and about this magazine woman, too. I hoped Sebastian wouldn't be there. I just knew he'd say something mean about getting rid of me. And I'd say back, "Yeah, well, sticks and stones can break my bones, but words will never hurt me." That'd show him.

On the streetcar, Joe said, "You know, Rebby ..."

My spine stiffened, because when Joe called me "Rebby," he was going to say something I didn't want to hear or cajole me into doing something I didn't want to do.

"I've been thinking maybe we shouldn't mention the move just yet. To Mrs. Martino, I mean. She'll get upset and we should spare her that."

"Are you saying we have to skulk away in the middle of the night again?"

He looked annoyed at my lack of sugar-coating.

"Of course not, Rebby. I mean ... let's just hold off a bit. Okay? We'll tell everyone next week. Less time for anyone to be ... um ... sad."

I could tell with all the hesitations, he was thinking this out as he went. I could also tell, being an old hand at the way his mind worked, he was only pretending to be concerned about my friends on Sullivan Street. His real motive, as always, was to keep people from asking nosy questions.

And so I nodded. And my nod was enough for him to think I was agreeing with him, but I was doing no such thing. Personally, if people wanted to be sad at the thought of me moving away, I was all for it. Why shouldn't people miss me? Why shouldn't someone throw me a small party and maybe give me a parting gift? This seemed to happen to normal people. Why not me?

I note I have written "normal people" in this last bit of writing but, of course, I had no idea what "normal people" actually meant, not being one myself—not that I knew this, either. It was Phoebe who told me later that whatever you grow up with—whatever is bred in your bones—is what you think is normal. And when you discover it isn't normal for anyone else, that you are, in fact, an oddball, it is a little bit like standing on an earthquake fault line and feeling the ground shift beneath your feet. But then, seeing my distress, Phoebe smiled and said, "Personally, honey, I have never given a flying ... fudgesicle about what anyone thinks is normal."

Where I've Lived

It usually didn't take much for us to move. In almost twelve years I had collected very few possessions, mostly because if you move around as much as we do, living the shabby way we do, you just sort of leave things behind and get new things at Goodwill or the Salvation Army. Joe always said, "Don't be sentimental," and I guess he was right. There is no need to be all clingy about chipped cups and tarnished toasters and second-hand stained sheets. (That last bit is called a litter-aye-shun alliteration.)

Most of the places we've lived in came furnished—or so the ads claimed. The furnishings sure didn't look like anything in decorator magazines. There was usually a bed and some wobbly tables and dressers and a hotplate and small fridge. Joe always took a look around and, with his hands on his hips said, "Nothing we can't fix up!" He'd go off to the nearest dollar store and come back with a bunch of cleaners and get to work polishing and disinfecting.

One place we stayed in for only two weeks because it had cockroaches. I'd never seen a cockroach before, but I'd read about them, and when I saw the shiny brown bug scuttle across the kitchen counter, I just knew in my gut it was a cockroach. I yelled and Joe came running and after that we saw lots of cockroaches on the counter and crawling out from behind the bathtub faucet.

The first place I can remember had an attic. I remember going up a ladder to a hole in the ceiling and looking out a tiny window down to the sidewalk. Joe said we never had an attic. "You're probably thinking of the Little Princess book." And I remember a cabin with log walls and a stove, but Joe said I must have read that, too. "You probably got confused with those Little House books you love so much."

To mollify me with each move (which means pacify, kind of like a baby with a soother in her mouth), Joe gave me money and let me go shopping for new things at the closest thrift store. I'd lug a hodgepodge of dishes and cutlery and lamps and knickknacks back in a wagon and then begin decorating. I felt a bit like Arrietty in *The Borrowers*, lugging home my finds.

We never hired a moving van like normal people do because we didn't have big furniture. Once I had a rocking chair that was my special reading spot, but when Joe woke me up in the middle of the night and whispered, "Let's go," we had to leave it behind. We got on a bus and even slept on the bus, and I remember waking up to see an island called The Sleeping Giant.

Once we lived in a place with a huge goose statue. We didn't stay long. Joe said we were going to try Toronto. He said he knew people there who really needed his expertise and had lots of work for him. And he said it was a safe place now, but I didn't know what he meant.

And then we ended up on Sullivan Street, which was a whole different ball game. (An aside: that reminds me— Mr. and Mrs. Wasserman took Jordan and me and her three brothers to see a Blue Jays game in July and we saw Roy Halladay pitch, and although I didn't much understand baseball, everyone else thought they'd died and gone to heaven. Sebastian sat behind me and kept dropping popcorn on my head. The dome roof was open and I got terrible sunburn, and Mr. Wasserman bought me a Blue Jays cap.)

We lived on Sullivan for the longest ever that I could recall, and I had a vast accumulation of important belongings, including many objets d'art (that is French for my collection of precious items). Joe gave me lots of money to spend. Not an allowance, exactly. But once or twice a week he'd give me five or even ten dollars. And if I had money left over from buying books or candy or going to a movie, I'd buy nice things I found in rummage sales or thrift stores. And if we absolutely had to move away from Sullivan Street, well, I would absolutely NOT leave one solitary possession behind!

Two Fights

After seeing the beige place, we got off the streetcar at Spadina, and on the walk north to Sullivan Street, I was thinking how to go about letting people in on the move without incurring Joe's wrath. I could say to Mrs. Martino, "I've got a secret," but Joe would know what I was up to and give me the dead bug look.

As we opened the latch on the front gate, Joe squeezed my arm. I thought he was distraught because he pinched a bit.

"Remember, Rebecca, not a word. Remember what we were forced to do last time."

Ah. A threat. It was always ominous if he called me Rebecca. By "last time," he means when we snuck away when everyone was at work and I didn't get the special cake and going away gift the landlady, Mrs. Tokiwa, promised me. I'm pretty sure it was the silk scarf I drooled over so many times. Joe said it was my own fault for divulging our plans before he wanted to.

So now, what to do? I didn't want to leave Sullivan Street any sooner than necessary, even though I was bursting to find out more about the lady spy (as I called Phoebe then) at the beige abode.

As we got into the tiny communal foyer, Mrs. Martino flung open her door and started yelling. An Italian woman yelling is something to behold. I enjoyed it immensely because she wasn't yelling at me and I could appreciate the operatic performance. It was Joe she was furious with. Or I should say, it was Joe with whom she was furious. (It is of extreme importance that all concerned should note that I am familiar with correct grammar.)

I have to admit I really liked seeing Joe getting such an earful. Maybe it isn't right, but what kid doesn't want to see an adult get in trouble sometimes? I mean, why should it always be the kid? And so, I was secretly thrilled when Mrs. Martino blasted him, half in English, half in Italian, waving her arms, tugging at her hair, hitting her forehead, pounding her chest. Begging him the whole time not to take me away from her. She put her arms around me and pulled me into her bosomy body and started to cry.

The fun was gone as I realized how much she liked me—really liked me—and how much I would miss her. Mrs. Martino was like a mother to me.

I glanced at Joe. He didn't look moved one bit. He looked annoyed. Annoyed with the new superintendent who, we found out, had phoned for a reference. Annoyed with Mrs. Martino for interfering. He stared out the front door with his trademark sulky glare, like a big baby. It was obvious Joe was thinking only about himself.

It was at that very moment I started to hate him.

Joe stalked upstairs. Mrs. Martino kissed the top of my head and I said I had to tell Jordan. If I stayed there, with her holding me, I wouldn't be able to not cry.

Jordan lives the next block over and has beautiful blonde hair that stays right where she puts it. Mine is black and kind of frizzy and flops every which way. And her clothes look like they were made just for her. Her family owns a dress shop on Spadina, so everything is new and gets altered. Sometimes I wonder why she likes me.

Her stupid brother answered the door. "Hey, Jordie! It's your weird friend."

I wanted to tell Jordan alone, but Sebastian followed us into the kitchen.

"Don't you have somewhere to be?" Jordan asked him.

"Nope. I have to be right here in the kitchen. I am desperate for chocolate milk."

Jordan rolled her eyes. Sebastian took forever to pour and stir and sip.

"Oh, for Pete's sake!" I gave up. "I'm moving, Jordan. That's what I came to tell you."

She didn't look as heartbroken as I expected.

"Oh! When are you going?" She sounded more like I said I was going on a trip, not moving away.

"In two weeks." I waited for her to ask more questions but she didn't. So, I told her about the apartment. "You can come visit me. It's not too far away. We could go on a hike in High Park. Joe said ..." I stopped because Jordan had a funny look on her face. "What? You got a stomach ache?"

"I don't want to, Reb. I ... I don't like Joe. He gives me the creeps."

"What do you mean?"

Jordan shrugged. "Nothing. Just, he's creepy."

Joe was odd, for sure. But creepy?

"He's so moody and he never smiles, and he doesn't look at me when I'm over and ... and if I say something, he tells you to tell *her* ... whatever it is. Like I'm not there or don't understand English. I told my parents and they think ... they think it's kind of weird. What you do."

"What? What do I do?"

Jordan banged the table. "Oh, come on! You don't go to school. You walk around all day by yourself. You don't have any family. You dress like a homeless person. My mom said not to hang around with you too much."

"Your mom said that?"

Jordan took a deep breath. "It's not that she doesn't like you. She does. My whole family likes you. Even Sebastian does. Right, Sebastian?" She looked at her brother but, for once, he didn't say anything stupid. He didn't look at me, either. "It's just ..."

"What?"

"What I said. You're ... you're not normal. You and him. But it isn't you. It's him. I don't ... I don't like being around him. I feel scared."

I did not know what to say. I kind of agreed with her, especially about the "normal" part, but she was talking about Joe, my dad, after all, and some bit of loyalty surged through me. And for some reason, some stupid reason I see now, I got mad.

"How dare you! I'll ... I'll never speak to you again! Cross my heart!"

"Don't say that, Rebecca! Please! Please don't be like that. We can visit. Just not with him. I'll miss you! We both will. Right, Sebastian?"

Sebastian finally came to life. He choked on his milk and made a gagging noise.

"Well, I won't miss *you*, Sebastian Wasserman!"

"Mutual."

And I left, shaking, wondering if Jordan was right.

The Truth of My Birth

When I got back from Jordan's, Joe said he thought it would be best if we went out for supper. He said he couldn't put up with Mrs. Martino banging her pots around for the sole purpose of annoying him. "Mr. Martino should make her behave."

So we walked up Spadina to Peking Garden Restaurant, and I ordered my favorite, the Number Eight Special.

"You'll have the Number Five Special."

"I don't like Number Five. I don't like mushrooms."

"I know what's best for you. Two Number Fives, Mr. Chang."

Mr. Chang glanced at me but he didn't say anything. When the food came, I picked at the bits I did like. Maybe I was crazy, but I thought there were more shrimp than usual and fewer mushrooms. Did Mr. Chang do that on purpose? Was he sorry for me?

Of course, Joe noticed me pushing my food around the plate. "Not hungry? That's okay. You're getting chubby."

I looked down, blinking back tears, and concentrated on eating. But why was I weepy? This was happening more and more often lately, especially when he said something mean.

"Why are you mad at me?" I asked.

"The proper word is angry, not mad. But I'm not angry, Reb. Just disappointed."

This was worse. "Why?"

"You know why."

"But I don't! I really don't know."

"Well, for starters ... how many times have I asked you not to spend time with Jordan?"

"Oh."

"And yet, as soon as we got home from the new apartment, you ran off to see her, didn't you?"

"I wanted to tell her we're moving. That's all."

"Fine. After we move, you won't see her again. Right?"

"What?!"

"Keep your voice down and answer me. Right?"

"Right," I mumbled. I wished I could say, "It's okay, Joe. The Wassermans don't want their daughter hanging around you!" Thinking that emboldened me. I shoved a mushroom under a hunk of bok choy and said, "You promised to tell me about my family. That is, why I don't have any. And I want to know right now. In one day, you made me give up my friend and my home. So ..." I thought I'd better shut up and see what happened.

Big sigh. "I met your mother ..."

I interrupted. "But you didn't meet my mother. You met Diana. She wasn't my mother when you met her." He looked exasperated, but I think it is important to get the facts straight, especially when there are so few of them.

"Well, at least I've done one thing right. You have a logical mind."

Gee. Only one thing?

"Continue," I said majestically, waving my chopstick like a conductor's baton.

"We were sixteen. We met in high school. Grade 11. We knew it was love. Love at first sight."

"How did you know that?"

"I'm not going into details."

"Why not?" I demanded. "I've known nothing about my life, and now you want to be miserly about details?"

My voice got loud, and Joe looked around and said,

"If you're going to make another scene, this conversation is over."

"Sorry," I mumbled and tried to look meek. No way I wanted to stop this flow of information—no matter how meager—until I heard everything. "It's probably so painful for you," I added.

"Yes. Yes, that is exactly it. So painful." He looked off to the side, sort of wistful, and I had my doubts. Looked like acting to me.

"Well ... she was beautiful and smart and funny and talented. We dated, saw each other all the time. Our parents didn't like it. Hers didn't think I was good enough for their precious Diana, and my family thought the same about her. So we snuck around and everyone thought we'd broken up. Then high school was over, and our parents assumed we'd go off to college, but ... oh, boy, this is the hard part ..." He looked around for a waiter and ordered a drink. "A martini, dry," he said.

I was shocked! I had never seen Joe drink before, and so I felt a tingling throughout my entire body. Whatever he was going to tell me sure must be something huge, I thought. At long last! The mystery of my birth revealed!! My heart pounded. (An aside: I also wondered how this woman could have been my mother. I was not, as I have mentioned, beautiful. And I wasn't funny and talented, either. I was pretty sure I was smart, but being homeschooled, I couldn't be certain. Joe didn't believe in the "farce" of exams.)

The drink came and Joe took a gulp, and then made a big production out of wiping his mouth and playing with the napkin and looking out the window. Finally, after a deep sigh, he said, "And then you came along."

"What do you mean: then I came along? You just skipped over a big chunk of time. What about the wedding?"

He looked up at the ceiling and then closed his eyes. "You came along and there was no wedding."

It took a moment to sink in. The earth opened up and swallowed me. I seem to recall the room swimming a bit. I asked if I could sip his martini.

"Don't be stupid."

I was going to tell him it isn't stupid to have a drink when someone is in shock. (An aside: Mrs. Martino let me sip wine when I was helping her cook, but something kept me from disclosing what I suddenly sensed wouldn't go over too well.)

"You were conceived in love. That means ..."

I cringed. Was he going to tell me now? Here in a restaurant? Over the Number Five special? Joe never talked about sex stuff, but I wasn't ignorant. In April, Mrs. Wasserman gave me a book called *Your Changing Body*. I don't know why she did, but it was interesting, I must say. I kept it hidden in a shoebox under a pair of embroidered slippers from Chinatown.

"Well, never mind what it means. Time enough for that. Diana was pregnant and we were happy. She was proud to be having my baby."

"And?"

"And what? There's nothing else to tell. Diana died. You know that."

Oh, no. Not this time. "You said you'd tell me why I don't have any family. I only know why I don't have a mother. And I don't know much about that, either."

Joe got his peevish look again, but he went on. "Fine," he snapped. "I was an only child and so were my parents. They had me late in life and now they're both dead. Cancer. No other family around. Diana was also an only child. Maybe she had aunts or uncles, but she never mentioned them. We ran away and lived very simply, off grid. She died giving birth to you. By then her parents had tracked us down and threatened to take you away from me. I couldn't allow that. Diana begged me with her dying breath to keep you safe from them. She told me horrible stories about how they beat her as a child, and how she feared for your life. So, when you were a week old, we ran away. I left a trail of false clues. But then her parents were killed in a car accident and it didn't matter about hiding anymore."

Stunned. That was the only word for it. Stunned. Dead relatives here, there, and everywhere. On the lam. My life was suddenly the stuff of high drama and soap opera. What to say? Where to begin? "Where is my mother's grave?"

"She was cremated. I couldn't bear to go through all the hypocrisy and chose ... well, actually ... she chose as she lay dying—one of those very simple rites."

"Well, where are her ashes?"

I saw Joe thinking. His eyes dart side to side a bit when he's trying to decide what to say ... or making things up. "I scattered her ashes over the ocean. From the ferry between Vancouver and Nanaimo."

"That's the Strait of Georgia, not the ocean."

He immediately looked peeved and I could have smacked myself—a tidbit of information and I almost missed it being such a show off! "British Columbia? Was I born in British Columbia?"

Joe nodded, but he refused to answer any more questions. Even when I said, "Mountain goat." He looked at me as if I were an idiot. "You know, we saw a mountain goat." And I felt myself rummaging around in my mind, trying to get a handle on a memory that was lurking just out of sight. "On the highway. We had to stop the car. By water. And ... there were mountains with snow and a glacier. Don't you remember?"

He sighed. "No. I do not. You're remembering a book or some movie. You were a few weeks old when we left."

"Why couldn't you have told me all this before?"

"I was worried about you. I figured the less you knew, the better. And I didn't want you feeling sorry for yourself."

Of course not. Not even when I had real honest-to-goodness reasons to feel sorry for myself.

I was confused by something else. "I get why you ran away at first, but why do we keep moving now? Why are you so worried about people being nosy now? I mean, if everyone is dead?"

He shrugged. "Old habit. I got used to keeping things to myself, just in case. Coincidences do happen. Someone could have known other people in Diana's family and mentioned running into us."

"But then we don't have to leave Sullivan Street! We're not really in hiding anymore. It doesn't matter if Mrs. Martino or Mr. Popolopolos asks questions about me. We can stay." I started crying. "I want to stay, Joe. It isn't fair. I want to stay. I like it there. I love it there. It's home."

He handed me a paper napkin. "Wipe your nose. We can't stay. I've signed the lease."

He continued. "Besides, it isn't about hiding from relatives anymore. It's about people sticking their noses into our business. I like homeschooling you. I believe kids should be allowed to roam free. Lots of time for institutions later on in life. Freedom from the man."

"What man?"

Joe looked annoyed. "It's an expression. Like Big Brother."

"I have a big brother?"

Joe slammed his hands down. "No!" He glanced around and saw a couple looking at us. "It's another expression," he said quietly. "I'm talking about the government. 'The man,' 'Big Brother.' Code for the government prying into my business. Dictating how to live my life."

"But ..."

"But ... the problem is, Sullivan Street is too chummy. Everyone knows what everyone else is doing. In our new apartment, nobody will concern themselves with our business. We'll be able to keep to ourselves, no questions asked. That's the beauty of a high-rise. Anonymity."

I don't know where it bubbled up from, but I was suddenly furiously angry. "And what if I want people to concern themselves with me? Huh? What if I want friends who care about me and invite me into their homes, and like me enough to ask questions? Huh? What if I don't want to be anonymous? Huh?" I gripped my chopstick so hard it broke in half.

He got up. "I'm going to the bathroom. Settle down." As soon as he turned, I grabbed his martini glass with the idea of flinging it at his head, but I wasn't sure what would happen if I did. Jail? The waiter came over to the table with a deep-fried banana and lychee ice cream.

"Your dad ordered this for you, Rebecca." Paul Chang smiled as he set it in front of me with a flourish.

I hate lychee ice cream.

I said, "Thank you," and waited till Paul left before dumping the bowl upside down on Joe's plate. I wasn't a child to be bribed with dessert anymore. I leaped to my feet and ran out of the restaurant, the broken chopstick clutched in my fist. I stomped in every big puddle from today's rain.

I knew I'd be in trouble. But I liked the idea of running away. It was in my blood—bred in my bones—my heritage from Joe. Served him right.

Impressions and Memories

Of course, I didn't really run away. And I knew Joe wouldn't be worried, either. Angry, but only because he'd have to explain to the Changs. He hated scenes. He hated anyone noticing us. I'd go back to Peking Garden tomorrow and apologize.

What I did was walk up Spadina and look in store windows. So many pots and baskets and rattan chairs, and porcelain jars and smiling Buddha garden statues, and beads and silk wraps and ... It made me yearn for a permanent home someday so that I could walk into real stores and buy lovely things—for keeps. Mine for keeps.

I hung a right on Dundas and let the fragrance fill my head—the glorious blend of the herbs and medicines and fruit and hoisin sauce, and incense and barbequed ducks hanging on strings in windows. I wished I could have lived above one of these stores. Even when it was garbage day and the street smelled of rotting fruit and decayed vegetables, and rats and mice scurried about. (They would all be Walt Disney rats and mice, of course, and possibly help me become Cinderella.)

Michelle was sweeping the sidewalk in front of her family's store. There was a poster in the window of Lena Ma, running for the Miss Chinese Pageant. She was very beautiful and she was Michelle's idol. She hoped one day to enter that contest herself.

"What's wrong, Reb? You look upset."

So I told her what I did, and what Joe had told me about my family. "And my grandparents, all four of them, are dead."

"All at once? You mean an accident?" Michelle looked so shocked I actually laughed, which wasn't the reaction she was expecting.

"No. I meant I just found out they've been dead for some time. Joe never told me before. Thought it would upset me. As if finding out all at once wasn't worse. I mean, he could have sprinkled their deaths over time. One a year, say."

"I guess with your mom dead, too?" Michelle offered as an explanation for Joe's thoughtlessness. She held out a mango. "I have all my grandparents here." Michelle flapped her hand toward the apartment over the store. "They all came from Beijing together. They watch out for me every second."

I glanced up at the windows and wondered if a grandparent would say something about Michelle giving away the family's produce, and I thrust the mango into my backpack. Then I pondered the ramifications of having four grandparents aware of my existence. I was pretty sure life would be very different.

Michelle picked up the broom. "Back to work. But I'm sorry, Reb. Sorry you lost all your grandparents, I mean."

"'To lose one parent may be regarded as a misfortune. To lose both looks like carelessness.' Oscar Wilde wrote that. In *The Importance of Being Earnest*. It's a play. He was being silly."

Michelle laughed. "You're a funny one, Rebecca."

I walked along Dundas Street, planning my arrival home. Too soon wouldn't be dramatic enough, but too late and Joe might be really difficult to live with for a few days. So, I stopped to check out the exhibits at the Art Gallery and thought I'd like to see the Modigliani one when it came. He's an Italian painter and I thought maybe Mrs. Martino might want to come with me. I liked the way he drew people and even tried copying his style. Joe approved of this sort of thing, said it was edifying, by which he meant it was good for me. (I looked it up.) I tried copying Picasso but I didn't understand Picasso.

Once I took a tour through the Impressionism gallery. The guide explained that the camera got invented back then and so painters didn't have to paint people and gardens exactly as they looked. If some hoity-toity wanted a picture of himself, he got a photographer instead of a painter. So, some painters began painting their impressions of things—their first impressions, before their brains took over and told them what they were seeing. And since a lot was happening with science in those days, and apparently objects weren't as solid as they seemed—atoms and such—the artists tried to capture this shapeshifting of molecules.

When the guide finished talking, I wanted to ask some questions, but the teacher in the group was looking at me funny, and I guess it finally came to her attention I wasn't one of her paying students.

So I went to the Gift Shop and bought a poster of a Van Gogh painting—Irises. They made the poster in 1981 for an exhibit. When I put it up on my wall, Joe said he'd seen that exhibit. He was in Grade 9 and they went on a class trip.

I liked learning about Impressionism for two reasons. First, it made me think my life wasn't so odd after all. If reality isn't fixed—no one size fits all—well, then, maybe there was an explanation that fit me.

And second, when I told Mr. Popolopolos, it shut him up. He saw me in Yee's Emporium at eleven one morning and began his usual lecture. "Why aren't you in school?"

"But Mr. Popolopolos, you know I'm homeschooled."

Snort. "Then why aren't you at home?" He looked around. "Where's your dad?"

I showed him the color pastels in my hand. "I'm getting art supplies for a project. I'm studying Monet at the moment. He was an Impressionist." When I saw Mr. Popolopolos look flummoxed, I told him about the invention of the camera. He narrowed his eyes and shook his head. "I don't like it," he said. "You spend far too much time alone. I've a good mind to call the school board."

Did I? Did I spend too much time by myself? Joe sure wasn't handing out much work lately. But that wasn't my fault. And I knew that if Mr. Popolopolos called the school board, Joe would blame me.

The thought of Joe blaming me reminded me of what I'd just done in Peking Garden, and I knew I'd be in trouble. That word—trouble—sort of echoed in my head for some reason. Suddenly I had a memory. So fleeting, I almost couldn't catch hold of it. An impression! I was on a sidewalk ... a wet sidewalk ... wet cement. And I stepped into the wet cement ... red rubber boots ... and a verandah ... and a woman with black hair ... and she said ... "You'll get in trouble!" And she picked me up and I was looking over her shoulder and could see the footprints in the cement ... and ...

And it was gone.

Was that me? Who was the woman? Where did this happen?

I sat down on a bench and I had this weird ... I don't know what it was. I was little and I was scared. Why? I was saying, "Where's Mommy? I want Mommy." Why? Then it was gone. Like the lady with black hair. Gone.

I shook my head and stood up. I wanted to stay out a bit longer, but I also wanted to ask Joe about the cement memory. So, I ambled down McCaul Street, past the crazy table-top art college, and cut through the park to home.

"Hey!" someone shouted behind me. "I said hey! Hey, weird-o!"

Sebastian! I wheeled around, hands on hips. "Are you following me?"

"I didn't know it was you. Or I wouldn't have reported an alien sighting."

Oh, I hated Sebastian Wasserman! "What are you doing out? Isn't it past your bedtime?"

"Hardy har-har. What were *you* doing at the Art Gallery? You're too dumb to appreciate art."

"I am not! I study art all the time, so there. And I'm going to buy tickets to see Modigliani, for your information."

"Well, for your information, Miss Know-It-All, you don't say Mo*dig*liani. In Italian, the 'g' is silent. Modeeleeanee."

I wanted to hate him even more but ... "How did you know that?"

"Everybody knows that. I mean, if you go to a *real* school."

I knew he was goading me. But instead of telling him off, I got weepy. Again. I turned around so he wouldn't see. And he rode away on his bike before I could think of some awful insult back.

I got home and Joe was reading a newspaper. He made a big show about not looking up. Normally I would have ignored him, too, but now I had this pressing need. So I apologized quickly and, before he could begin about behaving in public and not calling attention blah blah blah, I launched into my memory.

He had the newspaper up again, and I saw his fingers tighten around the page. "I have no idea what you're talking about."

"But you must. Who was the woman? She had black hair."

"You must have dreamed it. Or ..." I could tell he was thinking. "Or it might have been a babysitter. A neighbor." He turned a page, clearly dismissing me.

"But what about the wet cement? Wouldn't that woman have showed you what I did?"

"No idea. Not very important stuff, Reb."

"Well, it's important to me. It is part of my life."

When he didn't respond, I went to my bedroom. I slammed the door, but without much energy. I thought I might be overdoing things a bit in one night.

In seconds, he opened my door.

"What are you reading?"

I held up my book. "*The Diary of Anne Frank*."

"I want a book report by Thursday. You've been lazy lately. Maybe that's why you're misbehaving."

The injustice of this was unbearable. "I am *not* lazy.

I read every day. You're the one who hasn't assigned any work."

"Well, when we get to the new place, all that is going to change. Discipline. That's what you need." He walked out.

Discipline! As if. He was the one without discipline. He was the one who told everyone he homeschooled me but, lately, as far as I could figure out, I pretty much did all the schooling myself. I read and went to the museum and the art gallery and went to movies at the Revue on half-price day, and talked to people and helped out Mr. Chung, and and ... Oh! I was furious! So why on earth did I defend him to Mr. Popolopolos? I asked myself.

It wasn't always like this. When I was younger, we walked around the city and he read books and newspapers to me. When I got a little older, he'd make me read three different papers' account of some event, and then I had to write a report about it. He wanted me to understand bias and how the people (by which he meant "you and me, buddy") were being duped by powerful agents. I grew up believing I was in a spy movie, and one day I purchased a man's fedora and wore it everywhere until I couldn't find it.

"Did you take my fedora?" I asked him.

"People were staring at you," he answered.

But the last time we did anything remotely educational together was at the end of May, when we joined in the protests on the anniversary of the Tiananmen Square massacre. Joe made me read about what happened fifteen years ago and write about it.

I didn't think any of this kind of schooling was strange or unusual because I'd read *Parvana's Journey*. Her father taught her because she couldn't go to school on account of not being a boy in Afghanistan. And that book led me to *To Kill A Mockingbird*, and I loved how Scout curled up in Atticus's lap every night as he read the newspaper to her.

So, for a long time, I was in very good company. My friends were characters in books, but still ... I never felt lonely or strange or different.

It was my normal.

And now, all of a sudden, I'm not working hard enough? I'm eleven, almost twelve, and I'm supposed to be teaching myself all day long? Oh! The injustice of it all! And where did he go every day? Whenever I questioned him about his job, he answered in very vague terms.

"You said we came to Toronto because of your expertise. What is it? Your expertise?"

"You wouldn't understand."

I know we had money for stuff, not much, but enough for cheap clothes and meals and rent. And the money he gave me. But how did he get the money? After tonight, after telling me about my family all being dead, I knew he wouldn't open up about anything else for a long time. So ... the next day, I followed him.

Joe's Job

I waited until I heard him leave, then raced down the stairs and out the door. I hid behind Mr. Martino's beefsteak tomato plants until he was a few houses along.

If he turned back and saw me, I would run toward him, begging for money to buy a book. He'd hand me maybe $5. You can get a lot of books for five bucks at a secondhand shop.

(An aside: sometimes Joe said I should take back some of my books and resell them and get money for more books that way. But no way was I EVER going to part with a book once I owned it. Another aside: this may have been the reason I didn't mind about not having a library card. Joe said I couldn't have one because he didn't have a driver's license, and you needed one to be able to borrow books. He then said this was more government propaganda to keep the poor out of libraries. But when I was old enough to understand that a library only let you borrow books and not *keep* them, I stopped pestering him.)

He turned onto Spadina and sprinted as he saw a streetcar glide to a stop. I couldn't run as fast and, even if I could, I certainly couldn't hop on the streetcar and let him see me. But another car wasn't far behind and I ran for that one. I got on and began the tricky bit of keeping watch to see when he got off. I hovered by the driver and ignored him twice when he yelled at me to move to the rear. I put on what I call my blank face and pretended not to understand him. (An aside: I have found it is helpful to look stupid when dealing with adults.)

We went underground and into the subway station, and I shoved past the other passengers to see if I could spot Joe. I took a chance and went down the stairs to the Westbound platform. If I saw him on the Eastbound platform, I'd have to try this again tomorrow. I wouldn't be able to run up and over and down before he would be on a train and gone.

But I was lucky. He was halfway along the platform, reading the newspaper. When the train pulled in, I didn't get into the same car, but then I had to keep looking out the door to see where he got off. I got a lot of dirty looks from other passengers!

He got off at High Park Station and turned up a side street and approached a van with a bunch of ladders on the side. The driver got out and pointed and Joe grabbed a ladder and went to a house.

Was he a burglar? I saw him on the roof, throwing handfuls of dead leaves and gunk down on the lawn. He went all around the eavestroughs and, when he was done, he did the same thing at a second house. The driver gave him some money and Joe pulled out a piece of paper and wrote something.

By now I was bored and hungry. I went into a Tim's and ordered coffee and a jelly doughnut and went home. I did the same thing again the next day, but this time when Joe met up with the van on another street, he pulled on an old shirt and started painting the siding.

A handyman. Paid in cash. That was the big secret. His expertise. Why we came to Toronto. So why didn't he ever talk about it? Maybe he was ashamed? He poses as this high and mighty intellectual—much smarter than anyone else—so this could be embarrassing for him.

The Bridesmaid

I walked back to Bloor Street and decided to walk home. It was sunny, and I wasn't familiar with this part of town. I wasn't too far east of High Park when I saw a Value Village. I'd never been to this one before and they were having their half-price week. I felt an irresistible temptation to shop. I did have some money, hidden in the inner pocket of my jeans. Joe sometimes forgot how much he'd given me in a week and sometimes I pretended I'd spent it, but I'd saved it instead. A girl never knows ...

But right then I did know! I wanted to shop without Joe hanging around, telling me what to buy. If he could have secrets, so could I.

I walked up and down the aisles, fingering everything, wondering what the wisest, best decision would be. Even if I shopped without Joe, he wouldn't let me wear something if he disapproved of it.

I sighed and started to head back to the sweatshirt section when ... the bridesmaid corner! Pinks and mauves and tangerines and yellows and emerald greens and ... I was uncontrollably overwhelmed with desire. A mid-length rose dress looked about my size, and it had big puffy sleeves and a puffy skirt and a pleated cummerbund and a huge bow in the back. And it was only $5!

A woman saw me drooling. "Costume party, honey?" And her friend laughed. "Too early for Halloween!"

What did they mean? I just smiled and took the dress into the fitting room. Off with the baggy sweatshirt and baggy jeans, and I pulled the dress over my head and smoothed it down and thought I'd died and gone to heaven.

It was stunning. It fit like a glove. There was a drip stain on the front and some sweat marks under the armpits, but I did not care. This was the most beautiful thing I'd ever had on my body, and I was taking it. And if I could never wear it outside, so what? I'd sleep in it!

As I started to pay, the cashier said, "This color will look awesome with your hair and skin."

Really? I could look awesome?

"And there were matching shoes the other day when this arrived. Did you spot them?" She said she'd hold onto the dress while I went to the shoe section, but I grabbed my dress back. What if someone swiped it from the counter?

There was a pair of rose-colored shoes with a tiny heel on the size seven shelf. My size. Holy cannoli! What was going on today?! I kicked off my scruffy old runners and slipped my feet into these gorgeous shoes, wondering if I would be Cinderella or an ugly stepsister.

They fit and I bought them for $4. So, after tax, I still had eight dollars and I knew what I had to do. I walked along Bloor till I came to the big drugstore, and I went in and headed straight to the razors. Joe said he would tell me when I could shave my legs, but I couldn't wear this beautiful gown looking like a hairy ape! That's what Sebastian called me one day—a hairy ape. Just because Jordan started shaving a year ago.

I had no idea how expensive razors were! Even the throwaway ones. They came in packs of three or five and they had multiple blades and strips of aloe, and when I opted for a really fancy one, an alarm went off as I reached into the display. I screamed and threw my hands up in the air as if cops were surrounding me, and a sales clerk came over.

"That's just to let us know someone has chosen the luxury razor," she explained. "Is this the one you want, honey?"

I shook my head. "Sorry. I don't have that much money." But she looked so kind that I blurted out, "I've never shaved before. I haven't a clue which one to buy."

She didn't make fun or anything. But I guess if you work in a drugstore, you have to be kind. I mean, what if you get folks in with ~~hemroyds~~ hemorrhoids or ~~diarea~~ diarrhea or halitosis? You can't be judgmental or you'd probably get fired.

"Well, you can start with these cheaper ones." She held up a bag with ten razors in it. "If this is your first time, you might need all ten."

I laughed at her joke. Then she handed me a Handy Wipe and pointed to a jelly doughnut blob on my sweatshirt. As I was paying, she rummaged through a drawer. "Here you go, honey. A few samples for you to try out." She held up a fistful of miniature packages and dropped them in my bag.

Gifts! "For me? Thank you." (Why was I getting all weepy?)

"You go, girl. Have fun."

I fairly ran down Spadina. I don't think this is what

she meant by "You go, girl," but I was determined to have fun before Joe showed up.

I couldn't believe this magical day, because when I got home, Mrs. Martino said Joe phoned to say he'd be really late, and so Mrs. Martino said I could eat with them.

"May I dress up?" I asked.

She looked at me askance (that means like I had two heads), probably because she knew my wardrobe did not include anything remotely suitable for dressing up. But she said, "Of course, bella. I'll tell Vincenzo and we'll all dress up."

She smiled and pinched my cheek and I thought how kind she was and how kind everyone was to me today. I remembered Blanche Dubois in *A Streetcar Named Desire* (another play about adults and their unending ability to make themselves miserable). Blanche said, "I have always depended on the kindness of strangers." And I understood. Strangers are some of the kindest people I have ever met.

I smeared on the sample of rejuvenating face mask and sat on the side of the tub like they do in magazine ads and shaved—tried to shave—my legs. It took forever, and I ended up with a zillion cuts and blood all over the towel. When the bleeding stopped, I rubbed the sample cream self-tanner on my legs. I put on my rose dress and rose shoes and the sample lipstick and sample perfume and sample mascara, and I felt like a princess. Even though my legs looked a little orange and blotchy.

I made sure there was no hair or blood in the bathtub and I hid the stained towel. I could throw it out and get another at Goodwill. Joe wouldn't notice.

I walked downstairs and Mr. and Mrs. Martino gasped when they saw me—shocked at my wondrous transformation. How I wished dumb Sebastian could see me at my very best and be sorry he'd called me an alien.

We had homemade lasagna and pan-fried chicken breasts and loads of grilled vegetables. I helped cook after Mrs. Martino took my hands and gave them a good look to make sure they were clean. We had tiramisu for dessert, and Mr. Martino insisted I have a small glass of vino santé. That's wine for your health, he explained, and so it was good for me, even if I was only eleven. We listened to opera all through dinner and I heard stories about life in their hometown of Pisticci before the war and before—spit, spit—bastardo Mussolini. One song made me cry. I didn't know why. I couldn't understand the words. But the emotion!

"Ah," murmured Mrs. Martino knowingly. "Puccini. Only someone with a heart of stone doesn't cry for that composer."

"What are the words?"

"O Mio Babbino Caro. Oh, My Beloved Papa. She is asking her father to let her marry her lover. He disapproves of him."

I nodded. I understood—it was like so many fairy tales. And, of course, it was just like the story Joe told me two days ago about him and Diana. I asked to hear the song again and Mr. Martino turned it up very loud, and the ache in the melody gnawed at my soul.

When there was a pounding at the door, my heart pounded right along with it, and I just knew it would be Joe here to order me home. (An aside: why was I so certain Joe would be mad to see me dressed up and having fun?) But it was only Mr. and Mrs. Petovsky, and even though they did come to complain about the noise, they cheered up when Mr. Martino produced more wine, and they came inside. Mrs. Martino put on Italian polka music and, pretty soon, we were all dancing. Everyone took turns with me, and I finally kicked off my shoes so that I could stand on Mr. Martino's feet as he whirled me around and taught me the tarantella. We banged into furniture and knocked over an end table, but everyone just laughed louder.

I never had so much fun in my life. But then Mr. and Mrs. Petovsky left, and Mr. and Mrs. Martino got out photos of when they were young, and when they began to kiss, I thought it was time to go upstairs. Besides, it was midnight and I knew in my bones that Cinderella had to get home or else. Or else what, I didn't want to think about.

I hid my dress flat under my mattress and my shoes under a pile of clothes in the closet and got in bed.

And—I'm not making this up—I fell asleep thinking life might be much better without Joe.

Leaving Sullivan Street

A week and a bit after the dinner party, we moved. I cried, but Joe didn't care.

"Control yourself, Rebecca. You're behaving like a stupid girl."

"I'm *not* stupid! And I *am* a girl. So there!"

He smiled the bad smile. "I don't know what has become of my little Rebby." He turned his back on me.

Like an elastic pulled too taut, I snapped. "I'm growing up. I'm not your *little* Rebby anymore! I even have a bra!"

He swiveled around. "What? When did you get a bra?" He was very quiet, but he sounded as angry as if I said I'd killed someone.

Oh, poop. For some reason, he had this thing about women's stuff. Told me he'd decide when I needed a bra.

I decided to bluff. I rolled my eyes and said, "Just kidding, Joe. Geesh! How would I get a bra?" But I stopped my weeping because I had to keep a grip on my runaway mouth. Because I did have a bra. It wasn't fancy or sexy like the bras in magazines. But the day after the dinner party, Mrs. Martino asked me to go shopping with her for groceries. Except she had an ulterior motive. Joe gave me some money to buy vegetables and said to make minestrone soup for our supper. (An aside: when I was little, I thought it was Mrs. Strony's soup and I wondered who Mrs. Strony was.)

So, off we went but, instead of going into the grocer's, we kept walking up Spadina to Yee's Emporium. "You know, bella," Mrs. Martino said, "you looked so beautiful last night. Such a pretty dress for a pretty girl. But ..." She held up her index finger and wagged it. "All that jumping up and down with the tarantella ..." And she jumped up and down and grabbed onto her bosoms and made them jump up and down, too. "And your bosoms, theyza grow this year!" She laughed. "Too difficult for the men to see so much. Capisce?" (Mrs. Martino told me how to spell capisce.)

Well, no, I didn't understand exactly, but I was intrigued by where she might be going with this. Which was to the bra section of the store. She picked one that was called a sports bra. It was very no nonsense, but she explained it would hold me tight. I tried it on and it fit, so

Mrs. Martino asked Mrs. Yee to cut off the tags and said I'd wear it home.

Then she winked at me. "If your papa should see it, you can tell him it's for the exercise. For the jog. Then, he no mind."

"Oh, he won't mind at all!" I agreed. One more thing to hide, was what I was thinking.

Mrs. Martino bought it for me while I stared longingly at the other bras with lace and hearts and even little bits of jewelry. Some of them were called underwire and I wondered about this, because the picture on the box showed pretty women with their bosoms pushed up and out, and I thought the point of a bra was to keep you down and hidden.

"Bella!" Mrs. Martino called, and I put aside my curiosity. After we bought our groceries at Chung's, we walked over to Kensington Market. Mrs. Martino knew a shop where they sold bits of rind off the Parmigiano Reggiano cheese they grated. They kept the rinds for their best customers. You need a rind of Parmigiano Reggiano cheese for flavor when you make minestrone soup. But I swore never to reveal the store where we went because Mrs. Martino didn't want the whole world to know. "Let them find their own supplier," she admonished, sounding like a drug lord. (I know this from movies, not my life.)

Afterwards, Mrs. Martino had an espresso and she bought me a gelato—hazelnut, my favorite flavor.

So, you can understand why moving away from Sullivan Street was heartbreaking.

On the day of the move, Joe went out and I ate breakfast with Mr. and Mrs. Martino. Joe came back with the white van from last week, but I didn't let on that I recognized the van. We had some furniture this time, and I absolutely refused to be parted from my latest reading rocking chair. Mrs. Petovsky gave me an old suitcase she didn't need, and I was very grateful because it meant I could pack up my personal things in private without letting Joe see. (Usually we packed in green garbage bags.) I opened the suitcase and was shocked to find some small gift-wrapped packages. I looked up, confused, and Mrs. Petovsky smiled at me and said, "Open them later, child. They're going-away gifts and moving-in gifts."

The packages were for me! I thought they were hers and she had misplaced them. I felt stupid for not figuring this out, but then, no one—not even Joe—had ever given me a present.

I got lots of gifts that day. Mr. Martino gave me a

huge box of Italian Bacci chocolates (that means "kiss" in Italian) and Mrs. Martino gave me an envelope with a wad of five-dollar bills inside. "Shhh, bella," she whispered. "Just between us women. Sometimes we need a bit of our own money." I nodded. Right now, I really needed another bra. I'd been wearing the one she bought me every day for over a week and it was grungy.

Even Mr. Popolopolos gave me a gift, except it was a history textbook he'd written when he was teaching, so as a gift I felt it was lacking somewhat. "You're a smart cookie," he told me sternly. "I don't agree with your father's methods, but I think you'll turn out all right. Don't stop reading." (An aside: I know I've made Mr. Popolopolos sound gruff, but back in July when Greece won the soccer tournament, he had a barbecue for the neighbors and he was lots of fun! Of course, it might have been the retsina wine. Joe didn't go and said I couldn't, either, but I did when he went out. Retsina tastes like turpentine smells, by the way.)

"Never fear," I replied as solemnly as he. "I live to read."

Mrs. Martino hugged me one last time. "Arrivederci, bella. Till the next time. Soon, eh?"

I looked around for Ollie but didn't see him, and I

think that was just as well. I'm pretty sure I would have blubbered if I actually had to hug Ollie one last time.

Jordan didn't come. We hadn't talked since our fight. Or my fight, I guess I should say, since she really didn't fight with me at all. Sebastian rode by twice on his bike, but I did not acknowledge his presence.

And then, really, there was nothing left to do or say, and so I got in the van with Joe and we drove east along Sullivan and down Beverley to Queen Street, and west across the city until we came to the beige.

It didn't take long to get our stuff up the elevator—under the suspicious eye of the superintendent (whom I shall henceforth refer to as the witch). And it didn't take long to unpack everything and get settled. Joe wanted to go out for dinner, but I refused. He was being so obviously buddy-buddy and chummy-chummy. I saw through the entire charade and wanted nothing to do with it. He forced me to move and I have to pretend I'm happy about it? Uh-uh.

"Why don't you go and bring me something back? I want to fix up my room."

He agreed, and thank goodness for that, because lately I wanted less and less to do with him.

I unpacked my suitcase and found a hiding place for

my bridesmaid's dress and shoes and set out all the gifts from Mrs. Petovsky.

I opened them slowly, taking time to untie the ribbons and peel the tape back carefully and smooth out the wrapping paper. Got the weepies again.

She gave me a candle in a silver jar, a big tub of body butter, a lace doily for my dresser, a package of fancy, sparkly hairbands, and a manicure set. And for some reason, a stick of Dove deodorant. A card said, "Enjoy being a girl." (An aside: this was a clever reference to the time she and I and Mrs. Martino went to see *Flower Drum Song* at the Revue—it's a song in the movie.)

I got out all my collectibles. I had a small stand mirror with gold gilt around the frame. (It wasn't real gold but, when I was younger, I used to pretend it was and that I was a princess.) I had a teacup and saucer without chips and the cup had a kitten on it. I had a little tray that said "silver plate" on the bottom, and I had a bottle of Chanel No. 5 perfume. It was empty, but if I kept the cap on tight, then every time I opened it, I got a whiff of a scent beyond description.

I also had a badly creased poster of Audrey Hepburn. It was in rough shape because I had to hide it from Joe. I saw it one day in a used video store and I felt like I'd been hit by lightning. She was so elegant and clearly out of my league, but there was something familiar about her. Had I seen her in a movie? So I asked the shopkeeper her name.

"Audrey Hepburn. *Breakfast at Tiffany's*. A movie. Ya want? Fifty cents."

I had my dimes out in the blink of an eye. He rolled it up for me and I forgot about whatever my errand was and raced home and taped it to my wall. I wanted to stare at it forever. This woman with her black hair piled high on her head, held in place with an enormous jewel, and big earrings and a massive necklace and a black dress. How could anyone look like that?! And what would someone's life be like if they looked like that? The idea was staggering.

But Joe came in that night and did a double take when he saw my new poster. "Where the hell did you get it?" he demanded. I knew he was really mad because he never swears. "Take it down."

"Why? I like it."

"No, you don't."

"But I do! And lots of kids put up posters. Why can't I?" (The only kid's bedroom I had ever been in was Jordan's, and she had posters of Justin Timberlake and Michael Bublé and Jennifer Lopez on her walls.)

"Because it's stupid girl stuff and I won't have it."

"No, it's not!" I screamed. "You're stupid!"

Two steps toward me and smack! Right across my face.
My cheek stung.

Shock. He had never hit me. Never.

"Don't you ever talk back to me again. Do you hear me?"

I mumbled okay.

"I didn't hear you."

"I won't. Talk back."

He reached up and tore at the poster. Dropped it on
the floor and left. I heard him stomp down the stairs.

I ran to the washroom and splashed cold water on
my face. What if the red mark didn't go away? What if
people—Mrs. Martino—saw it and asked?

I scotch-taped my poster back together. I rolled it and
hid it behind my curtain.

Now, with him gone for pizza, I got out my poster and
put it on the back of my closet door under my robe and
towel. Then I arranged all my new objects in amongst the
old and thought it didn't look like much for eleven—soon
to be twelve—years on the planet.

But it was my birthday in three weeks and a bit, and
he'd promised to give me money so I could buy some

nice things. Pillows maybe? A proper dressing gown for lounging when a person doesn't feel like going out? I'd love one of those fluffy white sheep rugs, too. And a nice throw for when I'm reading and want to snuggle.

I was standing on our balcony, looking out over the lake when Joe came back. He joined me outside and stood looking over the railing, staring down at the pavement below. And even in the fresh air, I noticed how musty he smelled. Like he wasn't washing his clothes enough.

"Tomorrow, we can go for a hike in High Park. It's right up the street. You can practically see it if you lean out a bit," he said, pointing around the side of the building.

But the thought of leaning out over a balcony on the (unlucky?) thirteenth floor didn't appeal to me, and the truth is, a shiver ran up my spine. I went inside and, because Joe seemed contrite, I managed to be civil. He talked about all the things I could do in this new neighborhood, and I made a mighty effort to ~~faine~~ feign enthusiasm as we ate a pizza that wasn't too awful (after Mrs. Martino's homemade ones, I mean).

But in the morning, Joe got a call and said he had to go into the office and left before eight. Snort. Office. Yah, right.

Funerals and Magazines

Joe left and I decided to go out for breakfast. I found a place called All Day Eggs. I ordered two eggs sunny side up and sausages with toast and coffee. All for $3.95! The cook gave me a funny look when I asked for more coffee.

"Aren't you a little young for the java?" He gave me a wet cloth to wipe some egg yolk off my sweatshirt.

I told him I was Italian. (The Martinos drank a lot of coffee.) He thanked me for my fifty-five cent tip and I remembered to say, "Ciao, bello."

When I stepped outside I saw a funeral going by—a hearse and a truck with flowers and a limousine for the family, and then lots of cars following, each with a small sign that said "FUNERAL" stuck on the hood. They turned down a side street without obeying the red light, and I saw everyone let them do that, except for one driver who honked and tried to cut through.

"Moron," someone grunted beside me.

"But they went through a red light," I said, and this stranger explained the etiquette of a funeral.

"Cars are supposed to stop and let a funeral go by. Respect for the dead. The last ride." He talked to me as if we were old friends. "But some people are so stupid. Think they're so important." Then he showed me how to make the sign of the cross on my chest.

"You touch your forehead, then your heart, then your shoulders left to right." And I suddenly figured out what Mrs. Martino did all the time, while I thought she was waving her hand in front of herself and brushing crumbs off her chest.

I had been to one funeral in my life, not for anybody I knew. One day when I was sketching in St. Michael's Cathedral, a casket was wheeled in and the family followed behind as the mighty organ struck up. I got in line and bowed my head and walked down the aisle, trailing everybody else.

(An aside: I didn't look as out of place as you might think. I'd been to see a lot of old movies lately with an actress named Hayley Mills. In *The Trouble with Angels*, she wanted to be a nun, and after seeing the movie, I decided I wanted to be a nun, too, so I wore a black dress and a white scarf around my head for the next three weeks.)

I've digressed. (An aside: Joe said I did that a lot in my reports, and he put a red slash through those paragraphs, sometimes so hard he ripped the paper.)

At the funeral in St. Michael's, I followed along with all the kneeling and standing and sitting and praying, and the whole time I thought deep and sincere thoughts about the mother who was gone from me forever more.

Where was I? Oh, yes.

When the funeral cars had gone past, I walked along Queen for a few blocks. There were lots of little stores that looked interesting, including secondhand shops. And there was something else, too. There were lots of people who looked like they needed a bit of help to get by. That's what Mr. Martino called it whenever we saw homeless people, which sounded kinder to me than Mr. Popolopolos calling them career bums. I gave some of them change as I was being mindful of kindness just then.

Hoo, boy—I've really rambled on! But here's the point: no one paid any attention to me! And for once I was happy about that. Maybe I could live in this neighborhood and not have to pretend I had a day off or I was meeting my mom, or I was on a field trip or going to the dentist (not that I'd ever been to a dentist), or was on my way to school this very minute with a late note in my bag. (I even had a late note all ready, just in case.)

Dear Mr. Smith

Anastasia is late today because she had a doctor's appointment.

Sincerely,

Mrs. De La Fountain-Bleue

I was clever enough not to use my real name, you will have deduced. And I changed up my handwriting a bit.

So, with a carefree spirit, I shopped along Queen. One store had a stand outside with small pots of baby roses, and I don't know what came over me, but I bought a pink one. I've never had roses (or any flowers) in my whole life, but suddenly I wanted to heed Mrs. Petovsky's advice and enjoy being a girl. I hurried home and placed the pot on my lace doily and, after admiring it for a bit, I took the elevator down to the basement and began a thorough search of my new abode.

On the ground floor was a laundry area that looked pretty grungy and not really suitable as a place to clean clothes. (An aside: I only rarely did any laundry. I wore a couple of things until they fell apart and then I went back to Goodwill for new stuff. Except for my underwear. I did those by hand in the sink when Joe wasn't around. And I didn't have to do this too often, because there are lots of stores where you can buy ten pairs of underpants for $2, and I bought three packages at a time to last a month. I *never* bought secondhand undies, just in case you were wondering.)

I walked into the garbage room by mistake and it was none too fresh, and, as I backed out, I saw a pile of magazines, tied up with string. Which got me humming "Brown paper packages tied up with string, these are a few of my favorite things" from *The Sound of Music*. (An aside: Julie Andrews wanted to be a nun in that movie, but instead she married a baron and lived in a mansion until the Nazis showed up. And I had just read Anne Frank so I know more than I can stomach about Nazis.)

I grabbed the magazines, a big bunch of *Vogue* and *Elle* and *People*. I hugged them to me and hightailed it back upstairs. I wasn't sure if the witch would accuse me of stealing if she saw me. (An aside: is it stealing if you take garbage?)

I burst through the door. Joe was home. Early.

"What have you got?" he asked.

"Ah ... duh," I answered. I mean, really. Wasn't it obvious?

"I beg your pardon?" he said.

I rolled my eyes, but before I could answer, he was across the floor and grabbed my arm.

"Why did you roll your eyes? Why say 'duh'? What kind of behavior is this?"

He had the look on his face—the one that indicated he didn't know me and didn't like what he saw. My whole body went tight, wondering if he was going to slap me again.

"Answer my question."

"Magazines."

He grabbed one out of my hands.

"They're fashion magazines, Joe. They're ..."

"I know what they are. Junk. You won't read them."

"They're not junk! They tell girls how to look and how ..."

"I tell you how to look. Understand?" He didn't wait for an answer. He took my arm and walked me to the garbage chute. "Go on." He pulled open the hatch and watched me as I dumped the magazines. "Good girl. Here's five bucks for your dinner. I have to go back to work."

He got on the elevator. I watched till it said "Ground." I waited ten minutes, and then I went downstairs again. I went into the garbage room and picked up another handful of magazines.

In the books I like best, the heroine never gives up.

Lunch with Phoebe

The next day, I chose the most recent magazine and hid the rest in my closet. I laid them out like tiles and put a mat over top.

I went downstairs to the lobby. If the witch saw me and asked why I was hanging around, I'd say I was waiting for my aunt. I liked the idea of giving myself a relative. I perched myself on an old vinyl couch, noticing it was chained to the wall, and began my vigil of hoping to see my beautiful spy.

I was finished the magazine and had picked up several useful tips about shaving and plucking eyebrows (something else I was pretty sure I should be doing) when an old guy stumbled in, looked around, saw me, and came over to sit. His clothes smelled like urine and beer and he had three days of morning breath. I wanted to move away, but he smiled and that trapped me.

"New here? I haven't seen you before." He suddenly looked worried. "Have I? Have I seen you before? I wouldn't forget you, would I?"

(How should I know if he'd forget me? Everyone else does.)

I shook my head and got up. "I am new here. But I have to go now." I thought I'd better leave the building because what if I went upstairs and he followed? I wasn't scared. I've seen lots of men like him, but I felt a little squeamish. Nor did I wish to hurt his feelings.

"Sorry, sorry, little girl. Don't mean to scare you. I live here. Name's Doug." He belched and the fumes just about knocked me over. "Offsir Doug." Hiccup.

"Nice to meet you, Offsir Doug. I'm Rebecca." I bent down to pick up my *Vogue* and someone came in the door behind me.

"Hello, Doug. Having a good day?"

What a beautiful voice! I looked up so fast I practically gave myself whiplash! It was her, and she was as stunning as I remembered.

Doug smiled. "Hello, gorgeous. You're looking like a bottle of Scotch after a month in the desert."

She laughed and then looked over at me and slipped

her sunglasses down her nose. "I think we sort of met before, didn't we?" Then she stretched out her hand and said, "I'm Phoebe."

I took her hand and felt awful because her hand was soft and her nails polished and my hand looked like I washed dishes all day in hot water and bleach. "I'm Rebecca. Rebecca Greene with an 'e.' I live on the thirteenth floor. Just moved in two days ago."

"I'z right! Knew hadn't seen you before. Never forget a face." Doug sounded like he'd won a contest.

"Doug used to be a cop."

I guess she saw the surprise on my face and added, "But bad things happen to good people. Right, Doug?"

Doug nodded and said it was time for lunch. And when he said "lunch," he winked at us.

Phoebe held the door for him, and I stared at her navy suit and high heels and red purse and scarf on her head, and when she turned back to me, I saw a quizzical look on her face. "You're rather ogling me. Have I got toilet paper on my shoe?"

I blinked and felt stupid and then for some reason, I blurted, "You're so stylish. That's all. I ... I'm sorry. I ... I'm an idiot." I knew I was bright red, but Phoebe laughed.

She picked up some mail and then got on the elevator and waved to me as the door shut. I watched, to note where she got off, and wasn't surprised to see the PH sign light up. Penthouse. Top floor.

I hung around the lobby for the next few days, hoping to run into Phoebe again. I had to be careful—whenever the witch spotted me, she demanded to know what I was up to, as if I had devious designs upon the building or the residents. And I didn't want her asking nosy questions about school. (An aside: Oh, my gosh! I sound like Joe!)

But I did see Phoebe a few times, and I always leaped (leapt?) to my feet to open the door for her. One day I was so engrossed in reading, I didn't notice she'd come into the lobby from the elevator. She asked what I was reading, and I jumped up and held the door for her and followed along with her as she went outside. I was telling her all about *Anne of Green Gables*, and I didn't even notice we were walking along the street together.

"I adore Anne Shirley," I said, "and she says she wasn't pretty. I'm not pretty, either, but I am smart like Anne, and maybe I could go to charm school and improve myself."

"First of all, charm school has gone the way of the dodo bird, and second, you are hardly unattractive."

I knew she was just being nice, but we were on Queen Street now and Phoebe asked me if I'd like to join her for lunch. We were standing in front of Mastro's and I was embarrassed I'd talked so much, and maybe she felt obliged to ask me for lunch.

"Oh, gosh! No! I mean yes, but you don't have to ..."

"Come on. I find I don't want to be alone, after all."

And next thing, we were sitting in a booth in a dark corner. A waiter (Tony) was there in a second, and only then did Phoebe take off her sunglasses. "What will you have, Rebecca?"

I ordered pasta fagioli with extra Parmigiano Reggiano and both Tony and Phoebe stared at me. "Where did you get that lovely Italian accent?" she asked. (So there, Sebastian Wasserman!)

"And how does a kid know about pasta fagioli?" Tony asked. "Are you Italian?"

It seemed simpler to say yes, but when Tony left, I let Phoebe know I wasn't really Italian. "Maybe a bit in my soul—or that's what Mrs. Martino used to tell me."

So, over some bruschetta, I told her about Mr. and Mrs. Martino and about Sullivan Street. "I was really sorry to move away, but now that I've met you, I don't mind so much."

"Ah. Flattery. I've seen you with your dad. Are your parents divorced?"

I shook my head and told her about my mother. "I was conceived in love."

She pressed her lips together and her face twitched like she was keeping in a sneeze. "You don't say."

"I do say!" I told her all I knew and then realized Joe didn't want me telling anyone. I asked Phoebe if she wouldn't tell anyone else. "Joe's touchy about stuff like that."

"I quite understand. We all have our secrets."

I wanted to ask about hers, but she asked me a question first.

"Why aren't you in school?" But she didn't say it like she cared if I was skipping (not like the witch). It was just a straightforward question, nothing nefarious lurking about its edges. And so I told her the truth.

"I'm homeschooled. Mostly do it myself. Reading, writing, going places." I could see she looked skeptical and I felt myself blushing. "Joe means well. And he used to do more, but he works a lot." Why was I defending him? "We're a bit low on money."

"Really? So you're on your own ... mostly? Any time for odd jobs for me?"

"Are you serious? Work for you? You mean it? Yes! But..." I realized I may have just agreed to be a drug smuggler. I wasn't naive. I knew there are criminals and gangs who use kids to do their dirty work. "Doing what, exactly?"

"Oh, odd chores around the apartment. Going to the store. Deliveries. That sort of thing."

Tony came with our bill and I said I could pay for myself, but she wouldn't hear of it. "If you work for me, an occasional lunch is part of the deal."

The kindness of strangers. Again.

On our way home, she took me into a couple of stores and mentioned brands she liked so I'd know in the future. She bought some Millionaire's Mix coffee (beans ground for a No. 4 cone filter) and a baguette from Rustico's (unsliced). Back in the building, I wasn't sure if I should stay with her, but she beckoned me with a finger, and we got on the elevator and she pushed the PH button. "How old are you? Do you need to ask your dad?"

"Eleven. And no. I won't ask Joe." I heard my mistake. "I mean, I don't *need* to ask Joe. He won't mind at all. And besides, I'm almost twelve. My birthday is less than three weeks away."

When the door opened at her floor, she said, "Want

to start now? More than simply carrying my purchases?"

I nodded, even though Joe had warned me about strangers who offered candy or kittens—and then kidnapped children. One day when we were on a bus, I saw a billboard. It was about a missing boy. There was a photo of him when he was five, and then a picture of what he was supposed to look like now, twelve years later, at seventeen. The bus was at a red light and I had time to read the whole billboard. It gave his name and his birth date and from where he was taken. HAVE YOU SEEN THIS BOY?

I tugged Joe's arm. "How can they do that? Age a child?"

He glanced out the window and scowled. "Tricks."

"But it's put up by the police. Or at least it says to contact the police. So it must be true."

"Well, it isn't. It's guesswork." He turned away and picked up the book he'd bought at a rummage sale.

I wasn't finished. "But it says it's computerized. So it must be real."

He sighed. "Right. As soon as they stick in the word computer, everyone thinks it's scientific. It's a scam to give people hope. And take your money."

The bus pulled away. "Why are you so angry?" But

he had given me the bug under the microscope look and didn't answer. Dangerously, I pressed on. "And how would I know anything about computers? We don't have one. Why don't we have one?" It seemed to me the whole world had a computer except us.

Silence. I switched tactics. "Still, it would be nice, wouldn't it? To think that if you lost a baby, you could find him again someday? Wouldn't you want that if someone kidnapped me?"

Joe pinched his lips together and looked at me, his eyes squinty. "The truth is, when a child goes missing, they don't find it. Or they find it dead."

I Get a Job

Phoebe unlocked her door and held it open for me. I had one last crazy idea about being kidnapped and never seen again and sold as a slave, and ...

I stopped, frozen, and stared.

"Ah ... can't get in the door, Rebecca. Mind moving?"

I came to my senses and stepped aside.

To see this, after all the beige and the shabbiness of the building. To walk into this after the dull, boring, blahness of all the places I called home. This was like ... like the time I found a jewelry box at a rummage sale and it was filled with dozens of old-fashioned brooches of every color of glass (which I had to leave behind when we made off in the middle of the night). This was stepping into an Impressionist painting saturated with pigment.

"Oh!" was all I managed.

"Like it?"

"It's wonderful!" There were leather couches and huge pillows and marble tables and tapestries and everything was red and orange and rust and yellow and gold and brown. And there were shelves of books and paintings and photos and … Slowly, I realized all the photos were of her, Phoebe. And in every one, she was with someone famous. Like the one with … "Oh, my goodness! That's Elton John! Right? It's Elton John!"

"Mmmmm."

"Who are you?" I finally asked.

"Can you keep a secret?"

I nodded.

"Because I'm keeping yours, aren't I?"

"Mine? I don't have a secret."

I put down the photo of Elton John and followed Phoebe into the kitchen (white marble), and she asked me to put the kettle on and make us tea. I wasn't certain if she was still auditioning me for the job, and so I made sure to let the kettle really boil and swish the teapot with boiling water and measure the tea leaves carefully, with one extra teaspoon for the pot. (An aside: it is not for naught I read Agatha Christie mysteries and knew how to make a proper English tea.)

She put a tin of chocolate biscotti on the counter and we sat on stools across from each other. She took a sip of tea and smiled. "I won't tell your dad you've been skipping school." She was watching me carefully. "Am I right?"

My mouth hung open and I must have looked like a goldfish. Finally, I managed to say, "But I'm not skipping. Really. Joe teaches me. I really am homeschooled."

"Then why aren't you with him or another adult? Why are you lurking in the lobby, day and night, waiting for me?"

"You knew?" I gasped.

She laughed then. "Oh, I'm not above a bit of fan adoration. But listen. I won't say anything about you, whatever the truth. And I am certainly not one to judge another's way of life. But ... do we understand one another? About secrets?"

When I nodded, she continued. "My secret is that in another life, I was a movie star. Xxxxxxx, (I've xed out her name), if the name means anything to you. I was young and suddenly had lots of money and fame, and people giving me everything I wanted. I was lucky. Not because of the fame, but because I survived, even though I got into serious trouble. Some of my best friends in Hollywood didn't make it out alive, and I mean that literally. I lasted quite a few years, though. Now I live here and keep a low profile, and my name, as far as the world knows, is Phoebe St. Claire. I don't talk about my past. But I could use an assistant. Often, I feel a bit fatigued. Does that appeal to you?"

"Yes! Oh, yes! I won't tell anyone. Cross my heart. Not even Joe. I promise." And I meant it. This was the sort of thing that only happens in books and movies, and you never believe it could happen in real life. Or certainly not to me.

She had her phone out. "What's your number?"

My mouth dropped. (Again!) I stammered, "I don't have one. Joe has a cell but I don't. No landline, either."

"Every kid has a cell phone now. Doesn't your dad need to call you? Know where you are?"

The truth of this—or rather the non-truth of this—hit me like I'd just walked into a door. "No. Never. He tells me when to be home and that's it. I do what I please, except for when he gives me an assignment or a chore."

"But ..." Phoebe looked confused. "Okay. We'll work something out. Are you around tomorrow?" When I nodded, she said, "I'd like you to pick up my dry cleaning and laundry. Here are the receipts and some money. And here's my key in case I'm not around or sleeping. I'll show you how to work the alarm."

And next thing I knew, I was outside in the hallway alone, clutching the key to Phoebe's apartment in my hand. I leaned against the wall and tried to breathe.

When I went back the next day with her clothes, she was home and I didn't need to let myself in. She thanked me and gave me five dollars and then she gave me a cell phone. "I have to be able to contact you." She showed me a couple of things about the phone and said I could figure it out for myself. "It's not a fancy, state of the art phone. Hope you don't mind."

I shook my head, afraid to speak in case I cried. But there was one thing I had to say. "Can this be another secret? From Joe, I mean? Somehow ... I mean ... something tells me he wouldn't like it. Not just the phone. About us, too. He ... he likes to keep to himself. He hates getting close to anyone in case they ask nosy questions. If I tell him ..."

If I told him, I knew what would happen. No matter what I promised to do (as in: "I swear on my mother's memory never ever to speak to that woman again! Cross my heart!"), he'd move us somewhere else as soon as he could. He'd have an excuse, and he wouldn't mention Phoebe. And I couldn't bear it, I couldn't!

I was afraid of Phoebe's reaction. Most adults band together against kids, (for your own good, they claim). But Phoebe grinned. "I understand exactly how he feels. I'm in hiding from the overly curious, too. But I understand you, Rebecca. I won't tell a soul."

The Party

A conspiracy means something sinister to most people, like Joe and his views about government, but the original meaning meant people coming together—breathing together—with a common goal. I know this because Michelle's father explained it when he took us to see the Dalai Lama speak about World Peace.

That's how I saw Phoebe and me—conspiring together.

I loved being around her. Not just because she was so pretty (I finally saw her without a scarf and she had beautiful shoulder-length black hair), but also because she was funny and clever and kind. There was that word again—kind ... the kindness of strangers.

Every day I climbed the back stairs to the penthouse floor (that way, the witch didn't notice the PH light going on if she was lurking in the lobby) and did whatever chore Phoebe had given me the day before, or to find out what errand she needed done straightaway. Sometimes she called me on my cell phone, which I hid in a book I found that is a fake book with a hollowed-out middle, and Joe didn't know. I kept it on silent (and checked every two minutes!) and I'd rush up the stairs when she called me. Usually she asked me to pick something up for her at the store or take something somewhere (she knew I traveled the streetcars and subways and didn't mind in the least). And it was sort of funny because, now, I didn't want to go off on my own all the time. I stayed home or close by in case she called. And because Joe was out so much, and was coming home late most nights, I didn't mind being in the apartment for long bouts. I only needed books, and I could spend the whole day on my own, reading, waiting for her summons.

One day she asked me to go to the library.

"Okay. But I'll need your card," I told her. "I don't have one."

"What do you mean you don't have one? I thought you read all the time."

"I do, but they're my own books. I buy them second hand. I'm not allowed a library card yet."

"Your dad won't let you have a library card?" She was arranging red and yellow gladiolas and glanced up.

I laughed. "I can't have one. You know that. I don't have a driver's license. Neither does Joe, so he can't get one either."

She put down the vase with a bit of a bang. "Rebecca, who told you that? Your dad?"

I nodded. "Yes. And ..." I stopped talking as something clicked. Joe drove us here in the white van the day we moved. Did that mean ... did that mean he drove without a license and could go to jail? Or ...

"Listen to me, Rebecca. You don't need a driver's license to get a library card. Just some identification, that's all. When you go to the library, ask about getting a card for yourself." She frowned. "Why on earth would he tell you such a ridiculous story?" She said it mostly to herself.

I knew the answer. We didn't have *any* identification, that's why. I found this out after Mr. Popolopolos lectured some people from his front porch because they wouldn't get up off their sorry butts and vote. Being Greek, he preached the joys of democracy. Joe said, "You'd think the old coot was a buddy of Plato."

"Why aren't you voting today, Joe?" I demanded. "You talk so much about the government. Don't you want to have a say?"

Joe answered that he didn't believe in the farce of elections.

"They're all rigged, Reb. They already know who's going to win. Those bozos are already chilling the champagne. But there is another reason, too. I can't vote because they ask for identification at the polling booth. And there is no way I'm carrying a government-issued identification card. Don't like snoops. Don't like the drones knowing my every move."

So, on the way to the local library on Queen, a few things fell into place. Joe paid cash for everything—he didn't have a credit card. In fact, I had never seen him even go into a bank. And then ... it was another one of those hazy memory moments. I suddenly remembered the money I'd found. When? I shook my head. Bundles of money with elastics. In a suitcase. In a closet. I leaned against the brick wall of a building. I was playing hide and seek with ...? And there was a big suitcase and I got inside and found dollars. And when I asked Joe, he said ... I squeezed my eyes shut ... "That's Monopoly money. It's a game." And I do remember playing Monopoly after that, but the money was different. "These dollar bills are so small," I said. "And they're all green. The first ones were different colors." And he said, "It's the latest version of the same game."

Then that memory blurred, but I remembered when I wanted to sign up for swimming lessons at a local pool, I had to give them my birth certificate. Joe pretended to look for his wallet, patting down his pockets, and discovered he'd left it at home. He told the clerk we'd be back.

I didn't care about Joe. He was a loner—I knew that by then—and it didn't matter to me how he wanted to live. But I needed some identification—something to prove I existed. And a library card was perfect for me!

I got to the library and decided to take a look around, having never been inside one before. You can imagine my surprise to see kids my age, sitting in front of computers. I felt cheated! All this time I could have been working on a computer and not thinking of myself as the only dinosaur still prowling the planet!

Then I wandered into a section for kids and saw moms and dads reading to children. One woman was reading a book aloud to a little girl in her lap and something ... something about it ...

"If you run away, I will run after you," she read.

I took a step toward her and stumbled, dizzy.

"Excuse me. Sorry, but what book is that?"

She glanced up and turned the cover toward me and said, "*The Runaway Bunny*."

And I had to sit down because I was suddenly a very young child and a woman with black hair was holding me in her lap and saying those words as I held a book in my hands—chubby baby hands. "If you run away, I will run after you," the black-haired woman said. And there was a bunny rabbit. Like a teddy bear, but a bunny rabbit. "Bunrab," I said out loud.

"Are you all right?" the young mother asked me. "Should I call someone?"

I shook my head. "No. Thank you. I'm ..."

She rummaged in a bag and handed me a juice box. "Here. You look faint."

Smile and say thank you and move away. Wonder again at the nature of kindness.

I got Phoebe's book with the library card she'd given me and asked about getting my own library card. The woman at the desk gave me a form for Joe to fill out. I thanked her and took the form and I chucked it into a garbage bin on my way home. Joe would never ever ever fill out a form.

I was almost home when it struck me—the black-haired woman again! Who was she?

The next day, Phoebe had lots for me to do. I ran about, picking up cheese and hors d'oeuvres and fresh flowers and macarons (an aside: do you know how much macarons cost?!?) and strawberries for a small party she was having that night. At her place, I got out serving dishes and dusted the living room, and she asked if I could come back later. "Just pick up dirty glasses and napkins and more or less keep things tidy."

"Should I get dressed up?" I had my fingers crossed behind my back.

"Do you own anything except old jeans and stained sweatshirts?"

That hurt a bit, but she was right. "You'll see," I told her.

So I ran downstairs and had a shower and got into my beautiful bridesmaid's gown. I blew my hair dry. (I had finally convinced Joe I needed a hair dryer and found one at a church rummage sale, and it only sparked a few times when I used it.) I sat waiting until the right time, and then I flew up the stairs in my bare feet to Phoebe's, carrying my gorgeous shoes so I wouldn't trip and could run faster. (An aside: the superintendent sure doesn't clean these stairs very often. My feet were black when I slipped into my slippers.)

Some of the guests were already there and, when I let myself in, they turned to look, expecting another friend.

"Dear lord," one woman said, staring. She turned away and I heard her giggle.

Two other people followed her glance and they both reacted the same way. And when Phoebe saw me, her hand flew up to her mouth. "Oh ... my ... God," she muttered. I didn't really take this in properly because I was wondering when Phoebe had gone to the hairdresser, because she had short red hair.

She introduced me and said I was a dear friend here to help. They smiled and one man shook my hand, and I went to the kitchen to work.

I hovered around the living room, waiting until someone put down a drink, and then I pounced on it and ran to the sink, washing the glass and putting it back out on the clean tray. I kept the cheese plate looking presentable (not like mice had been at it) and put out more crackers and watched to see nobody dropped a dirty napkin or spilled a drink on Phoebe's Persian carpets.

The music got a little louder and a few more people

arrived, but I didn't get introduced to them (because, like Cinderella, I was working in the kitchen), and when I went back out to the living room, a new guest looked at me and howled. (I say howled and not laughed because I think she was drunk.)

"What the hell? Phoebe?" And she pointed at me.

Everyone laughed and I saw Phoebe shoot me a look, but then, before I knew what was happening, one of the first guests said, "Phoebe! How clever of you! I just realized." And she opened a photo album and flipped to a page, and everyone gathered around her and they all howled. The woman called me over.

"Of course, you're channeling Phoebe here, aren't you?"

And I peered into the album and saw photos from a movie called xxxxxxxx and all the actresses had huge curly hair like mine, stuck out around their heads, and they wore big puffy dresses and ...

They looked ridiculous.

"I thought you'd never figure it out," said Phoebe. "Rebecca is brilliant, don't you think?"

And then she had me back in the kitchen. "They don't mean to hurt your feelings. They just can't believe anyone would willingly look as you do."

"Stupid. Ugly. That's what you mean."

"Don't tell me what I mean. You're a young girl, a pretty girl. Why wear this ... this ...?"

Someone called her and she left, and then ... I remembered Mr. and Mrs. Martino gasping when they saw me. And the two women in Value Village asking about a costume party.

I looked like an idiot. That was it. In fashion magazines, they'd call me a "Don't." With a black square over the eyes to protect the fashion faux pas from being recognized.

I wanted to die. I wanted to disappear. Why did I think I could ever be beautiful?

When no one was looking, I ran out the door.

Hair and Bras

I ran down the stairs, crying, carrying my shoes and I knew—KNEW—just how Cinderella felt. No. Cinderella fled *before* anyone saw how plain she was.

When I went inside my apartment, Joe was there, sitting at the table, eating. Why was he home early? It seemed to me fate had arranged this just so Joe could make fun of me, too.

He dropped his newspaper and pushed aside his plate and opened his mouth, but, for once, he was at a loss for words.

I did a little spin. "Pretty stupid, eh, Joe?" I taunted. (Best defence is a good offence.)

"Where ... what ..."

"Don't worry," I bluffed. "I haven't decided to go all girly on you. I was at a party."

"With who?" He was suddenly sharp.

"Just a couple of kids I met in the building. Nothing special." I pushed by him to get to my room. "And it's 'whom,'" I whispered under my breath. "With whom."

He was on his feet. "What did you say?"

I stopped and did my blank face. "Huh?" and then I sighed and made a sound that sounded like whoomm, like I was just letting the air out, hoping he'd fall for the ruse. I kept moving but Joe grabbed my arm. And I didn't know whether to be more stunned by the fact he was hurting me or the fact I could smell alcohol.

"What kids? How did you meet them?"

"Why? Why do you care? I hardly see you anymore. You're hardly around. So why do you care what I do all day?"

He stared at me and I stared back. "You're right. You're right. I haven't been around. I'm busy. Trying to earn some money for us to live. So, excuse me if I've been too preoccupied to dote on you, your highness."

His words stung, but I took the high road and shrugged. "Fine. But excuse me if I find some other people to hang out with. Kids. So there." I glared at him, and when he didn't say anything more, I turned and walked away.

"I hope it was an early Halloween party. Because you look like a joke."

I managed to get into my room and I banged the door shut. I panicked, thinking he'd come after me, but he didn't. I heard the front door open and slam.

Alone, I found the scissors and cut and ripped my dress to shreds. I put on my jeans and a sweatshirt and walked to the garbage chute, and I shoved in all the bits of bridesmaid's gown. I flung my shoes in, too, and listened to the clunking as they fell.

I went back to the apartment and ... where were my keys? I checked my pockets but ... Of course! I was an idiot! I had the keys in my hand when I threw everything down the chute.

It wasn't that late. I could go out until Joe got home. I had enough change in my pocket to ride the Queen streetcar back and forth, and that always took a few hours. And I loved doing that, seeing the neighborhoods and different people along this long, long street. One day in June I even saw Feist singing on a street corner! The thing was, that night, I didn't have any shoes.

And I could go to Phoebe's and ask for my key. I had a spare one made that I left at her place in case. But ... I did not want to go back there. I couldn't.

So I wandered around the building. I found more

magazines in the garbage room and went into the lobby to sit. I could have asked the super to let me into my apartment, but Joe had put on a safety chain without telling her (which was illegal) so she couldn't come in and snoop (which was also illegal). And if she let me in, she'd see it dangling. So, I read for an hour, and when I saw the PH sign light up, I ran and hid until the guests—I counted all seven of them—had left the building. Then I went upstairs and knocked on her door.

Phoebe was still dressed, but she'd kicked off her shoes and I could see she was tipsy.

And she was bald.

I looked down at my bare feet. "I'm kinda locked out."

"Uh-huh." She opened the door wide and I went in.

"Rather shirked your duties, my dear. Running out on me like that."

"You should have told me. You should have sent me home to change."

"Into what? Just what other clothes do you have? And besides, I didn't see you until you walked in. And later, when everyone was convinced you were in costume, looking like me in my diva days, well ... what should I have said?"

I sat down on one of her beautiful leather chairs and hugged a silk cushion into my body. "I thought I looked pretty. Joe said I was a joke. A Halloween costume." I couldn't look at her.

"Your dad ..." She shook her head and asked, "So? Why did you return to the scene of the crime?" She poured herself a glass of wine.

"The scene of the crime was in my room. I slashed that dress to bits and sacrificed it to the incinerator." I told her about the fight with Joe, that I think I dropped my keys. "I don't know when he'll be back. I don't know where else to go."

She got up and fished around in a glass bowl and handed me the key marked RG. "You know what I think?" She tapped the side of her head and, of course, she realized what was now revealed. Her hand froze in midair. "Ah," she said. "So now you know."

"You shave your head?"

"Cancer. Chemotherapy. I think I'll be all right. One never knows. But I do get tired."

"I'm ... I'm sorry."

"No need. Stuff happens. Of course, we all hope it doesn't happen to us, but, one day, it was my turn." She leaned forward. "Rebecca, I am grateful for your help. I couldn't have managed this party without you. But this is why my friends were shocked. They thought you were making fun of me—of my hair and clothes in that movie."

"But I would never ... I mean I couldn't ..." I had no idea what I was trying to say. So I cried and didn't say anything.

She opened a cupboard and pulled out a video. "So old it's not a DVD. Plop it in. You'll see."

We sat on the couch together, her drinking wine, me drinking—I won't lie—some white wine in a mug. (It tasted like sour apple juice, if you ask me.) I ate big handfuls of cheese and crackers because, despite everything, I was starving! And we watched one of Phoebe's movies. She was so beautiful!

She stood, yawning. "See you tomorrow. Noon? You've got lots to clean up."

But I tidied up lots right then because I didn't want her to see the mess the next day. And ...

Why lie? I didn't want to go home.

But I had to. I turned the key slowly, soundlessly, and snuck down the hallway and ... he wasn't there! And so I washed and got into bed as fast as I could in case ...

I didn't hear him come home. But in the morning, I found my rose plant with all the flowers snipped from their stems.

I carried the pot to the living room, where he was reading a newspaper. "You did this."

"You disobeyed me." He even smiled.

And the thought of him sneaking into my bedroom while I was asleep made me feel sick.

"Let's get something really clear. You obey *me*. Got it? You do what I tell you to do. Okay? You wear what I tell you to wear and you read what I tell you to read, and you *don't* talk to anyone I tell you not to talk to. Understand?"

I took too long to answer.

He twisted my arm behind my back and bent down to whisper in my ear. "I'm your father. You obey me. I'll ask again. Understand?"

The smell of his body and his breath nauseated me. "Yes." I choked out. "Yes, Joe. I understand." I went to my room and leaned against my door, my knees shaking.

I stayed in my room until I heard him leave, and then I let myself into Phoebe's apartment—she was sleeping—and I finished cleaning and wished I could live here forever. No matter how much I fixed up my bedroom, it could never look like this wonderland. And Joe sure hadn't done anything to the rest of the place. He slept on a futon on the floor and, other than a couch and chair and table that needed a book of matches under it to keep it steady, we had nothing in our so-called living room.

But I could forget all about my life because, for the next few days, I felt like I had found an oasis. I had no idea where Joe was most of the time and so I practically lived at Phoebe's, and we talked about all kinds of things as I did my chores. She talked about cancer and that was why she didn't like to go out so much, and how tired she felt and how she didn't want to find herself written about in the newspapers as "Former Star Battles Cancer," should anyone realize who she was.

"Of course, they'd dredge up all my past bad behavior and fall from grace, etcetera. And I don't need that sh— stress in my life now." I watched as she closed her eyes and took a deep breath and let it out very slowly. She did that a lot. That's when I told her about conspirators breathing together and she opened her eyes and laughed.

"You're laughing at me."

"Nope. Not *at* you. I think you're adorable. And I love all those big words you use."

So then I told her about the places I'd lived and about my Audrey Hepburn poster.

"And I hoped, I really did, wearing that dress, maybe I looked a little bit as glamorous as Audrey Hepburn. I mean, I know it's ridiculous. But if I don't look too closely in a mirror, I can pretend."

One day she asked me to help her sort through some clothes and then take them to this place that donates good clothes to women trying to get a fresh start in life. So, we went through dresses and blouses she said were just too revealing and too complicated to wear anymore, and then she put aside some bras—the most exquisite things I had over seen! She saw me pick one up—a lace one with beading—and I guess I looked covetous. (An aside: I know to covet is one of the seven deadly sins, but it must have been a man who wrote the list and knew nothing about ~~longeray~~ lingerie.)

"Will it fit?" she asked. "Yours if you want it."

I snorted! Of course, she had to know it wouldn't fit! What I said was, "They're beautiful! And brand new!" (I had bought myself another bra with the money from Mrs. Martino, but it was plain and boring.) "Why would you give them away?"

She seemed to tighten up and I thought she was—well, once I heard the expression: girding your loins. "I had a double mastectomy, Rebecca. A year ago. The party the other night was a small celebration. A one-year anniversary. So ... if you'd like a bra, please take one. Take them all! I don't use these ones anymore."

I wanted to say something, but what?

"It's okay, Rebecca. I've had time to make my peace."

I nodded and clutched the bra to my heart and didn't care if it would fit me now or ever! And I decided if it didn't fit, I would wear it anyway. And sleep in it, too. I did know that some girls stuffed their bras with tissue. Or socks. Jordan told me so. She had to tell me because of her stupid brother Sebastian.

One day he pulled a sock right out of her T-shirt in front of me.

"You idiot! I'm telling! Mom!"

Sebastian waved the sock in the air. "You'd better not tell on me, Jordie. 'Cause Mom wouldn't want to know about this, would she?"

Jordan went red and stopped yelling and Sebastian laughed. "How 'bout you, Reb? You wear socks for boobies instead of on your feet?"

Before I could answer, Jordan said, "Of course she doesn't, you moron. Her dad would kill her."

And for some reason, Sebastian stopped teasing us.

On Friday, Phoebe told me she was going away for a few days. "Think of all the catching up you can do on your schoolwork. You can't possibly be getting very much education these last few days. I'm taking up a great deal of your time."

I reassured her. "I read every day and I have to do a book report for Joe every week." I ran downstairs and ran back with my notebook and showed her. "See? I have to summarize the plot and describe the characters and talk about the theme and symbols and any poetic devices, and ..."

She put up her hands in a surrender motion. "What do I know? I've never had kids. It seems unusual, but clearly your dad is doing an excellent job." Then she added, "You know, you're very intelligent, but also naïve. It's an odd mixture. Enchanting, really."

Enchanting! Me!

But I said goodbye to her, heartbroken she was missing my birthday.

The Day Joe Said He Was Sick of the Sight of Me

I think I've written enough about life with Joe. Like I said, I think there were lots of signs my life didn't make sense. And I see now that adults *did* ask questions. But as Phoebe said later, it wasn't as if I was starving or had a black eye or a broken arm or too many bruises. So, nobody argued too much with Joe or called the police.

And so I'm back where I started, on my birthday, Sunday September 26th. And I'm ready to write about it now.

Joe and I were on the bus, going home from the book festival. I looked for a separate seat because I didn't want to be near him. But the bus was crowded and we had to sit together. It was a long ride and I didn't want to talk. It seemed weird to me that it was such a beautiful day. I mean, I was glad it was warm and sunny and not a cloud in the sky when I woke up on my birthday. But now, with Joe being so awful, I thought it should have been drizzling and gray and damp, with lots of thunder and lightning.

I picked at the bit of loose wool on my sweater until Joe reached over and slapped my hand. "Stop that," he said. He got up and moved. A woman across the aisle watched him and then swiveled around to look at me. Her expression indicated she thought we were weird. I shrugged and went back to staring out the window.

Were we weird? And how should I know? Something cold and hard was taking root in my chest, like icicles forming off a roof, drip by drip. He was getting sulkier and more difficult by the day. And he blamed me for it. My bad attitude, he said. My constant questioning of his authority, he said. He didn't mention the bridesmaid's dress today, on my birthday, but he'd made fun of me a few times last week. He said that, what with the mudslide in Haiti that killed thousands a few days ago, he was disappointed in me being so self-absorbed and conceited.

I started to argue. "How could me buying a $5 dress a month ago stop the ...?" I didn't finish. I didn't care. I didn't want to argue or listen to him. No matter what I said, I'd never be right.

He got up to take the crosstown bus to the subway. He didn't look back, so I didn't follow. I could go home another way. The longer way. I switched seats so he couldn't glare at me as the bus drove by.

He sprang up when I walked in and he was at my side in a split second. He yanked my arm and I felt the shock at my shoulder.

"What the hell do you think you're doing?" He didn't shout. And that made it scarier.

"Ow! Let go!" I pulled away but he held on and he pinched. I saw the bad smile.

"All day today you were a royal pain in the ass. Rude, sullen, disobedient. Then to pull a stunt like that, not getting off the bus."

"I am not rude! I ask you some questions and you act like you're guarding a secret vault. And you ignored me on the bus. You got off and expected me to follow like a ... like a sheep, so it serves you right!"

He brought his hand up then, and I knew he was going to hit me. I cringed and shut my eyes as I waited for the slap. But he dropped my arm and pushed me away so hard I stumbled. "Go to your room. I'm fed up. After all I've done for you."

I made sure the chair was between us. "What? What exactly have you done for me except run away with me?

We keep moving around and I never get to have friends or go to a real school or wear nice clothes. So, what should I be so grateful for? Huh? Huh?"

"I said, go to your room." His voice was flat. "You're an ungrateful bitch. Just like your mother."

The tears were hot and stung my eyes, but his words stung even more. What did he mean? Bitch? Like my mother?

"And you know what else? I'm sick of the sight of you."

He could say that? To me? On my birthday?

My head was pounding as I walked to the door.

"Where do you think you're going?"

"A friend's."

He was in front of me, his arm across the door. "What friend? The same kids at that party?"

I knew to lie. "Yes."

I tried to push his arm out of the way, but he grabbed my shoulders and his fingers dug in so hard I winced. "I said go to your room and I meant it. And you will not talk to those kids again. Understand?" He shoved me again and my head snapped back and hit the door.

I stood there, frozen. I looked at him, at this stranger. Lips pulled back from his teeth. His eyes the eyes of someone I did not know.

I managed to get around him, my shoulder blades squeezing like I expected to be hit. In my bedroom I sat in my chair and felt—what? Scared? Numb?

In minutes, he opened my door. He threw a ten-dollar bill at me and I watched it flutter through the air. "I'm meeting some friends. Get a pizza."

He walked out and I could hear him at the front door, and something galvanized me and I called out. "Joe! Wait! It's my birthday! Please, don't go. I'm sorry. I'm sorry! Please!"

"Don't much care, Rebecca, so save your tears. And you know I don't go in for phony stuff like birthdays." And he was gone.

It never dawned on me until then that we didn't celebrate his birthday. I didn't even know what day it was. Or how old he was. Surely that was strange? Why didn't I ask? All I can think of is that it was part of his refusal to let the government poke and pry.

I heard the elevator slide open and I ran to the peephole to see him get in and the door close. I smashed my fist into the door. Then I kicked everything in sight and screamed. "I don't need you! I can celebrate my birthday without you ... you ... stupid, selfish, rotten ... Bastardo!" Spit. Spit.

Mrs. Martino! Could I go to her? But what if she wanted to confront him? Would he listen to her? Of course not. But then ... but then what would he do to me after she yelled at him? And I thought of all my lovely possessions, broken and ripped. He would do it, I knew. My roses. And then, a few days ago—my magazines ripped apart. He went into my room and went through my closet and found them. So he knew I'd defied him. He knew I got more magazines after he made me chuck the first ones down the garbage chute.

So, could I keep it a secret from Mrs. Martino? Pretend everything was fine? But ... why *should* I keep it a secret? Why did I feel I couldn't tell anyone about what a terrible, childish father I had? Why did I want to protect him?

He's all you've got. I heard this voice in my head. And then began this back and forth tennis game in my brain as I tried to sort things out.

I knew I wasn't going to leave the apartment. I didn't want to be here, but I didn't want to go out into the world, either. I felt like one of those insects you see trapped in sap on a tree. Alive, but not really. And not for long.

I thought about Jordan.

She called Joe creepy. Now I knew she was right.

Creepy. That was the word for what I felt. When he came into my room at night. Like I was in a horror movie and the crazy person is in the house when you're alone. I wished I could talk to Jordan.

A sudden pounding at the door gave my heart a jolt. I crept over and peered out. It was the witch, but I didn't say anything.

"Open up in there!" she yelled, thrusting her eye against the hole as if she could see in.

I didn't breathe.

"I know somebody's in there, now open up!" She paused, then yelled, "Any more complaints from the neighbors and I'll call the cops!" She waited, her mouth pinched up tight, then marched down the hall. I didn't budge until she was in the elevator. Even then I tiptoed to the couch. Hoped the springs wouldn't squeak and give me away.

I sat in the dark and watched the sky fade to black and the lights came on in the city. The moon rose over the towers and none of it—not one light of it—was for me. Not even one birthday candle.

I didn't feel like shouting any more. Or crying, either, I realized with some sort of surprise. No family, no friends, no party, no gifts, not even a book bought at the book festival today. Not even the money he promised to fix up my bedroom.

There is a monument a block away. It is for Polish officers who were killed in the Second World War. It is a big black slab of stone and it is cracked in a jagged split down the middle.

That is how I felt.

My Transformation

I was curled on the couch and stiff. The sky was pencil-lead gray. Memory jerked at my mind and I jumped up. I looked over at Joe's futon. He wasn't there. I ran to my room, but he hadn't gone there to sleep, either.

He said he was meeting friends, but that was a lie. He didn't have any friends. Or none that I knew about. And how much did I know about him, anyway? I didn't even know when his birthday was! I mean, I knew he was about thirty, because they had me at the end of high school, which would make him maybe eighteen? So, thirty subtracted from 2004 and he was born maybe in 1974?

Something didn't make sense. I looked at the Van Gogh poster—1981. He said he went to this exhibit when he was in Grade 9. But ... but that would mean ... he was seven years old in Grade 9? Or ...

Or he lied. Of course, he lied! But which lie was it?

He lied about seeing the exhibit? Or he lied about when he was in high school? Was he really almost forty? But wouldn't that mean the story about him and Diana ... about me ...

Thirty-seven? Thirty-eight? Wasn't that old? But he didn't look old—not to me. He wore jeans and sweatshirts like me, and old running shoes, and he kept his hair long and ... I realized I hadn't ever thought about him this way. He was just ... Joe.

And ... and wasn't there something else? Something else I tried not to think about?

He said we left British Columbia when I was a baby. A few weeks old. But how could I remember a mountain goat if I was so little?

There had to be a simple answer. I would ask him when he came home. I never doubted he'd come home. I never doubted he'd talk to me again, in a normal way, after a lecture.

And in the meantime? Could I get through my day? Put it out of my mind? In Gone With the Wind, Scarlett said she'd think about it tomorrow. Could that really work?

I had a shower and ate cereal and went up the back stairs to water Phoebe's plants.

But she was home, back early from her long weekend. "Hello darling! How was the birthday?"

"You said you'd be gone until Wednesday."

"A slight change in plans. I'm leaving again tomorrow, and I'll be gone this time for most of the week. Now, tell me all about your birthday!"

"Oh ... well ..." I didn't have a story ready.

And when I paused too long, she said, "Rebecca? What is it, honey?" She put her hand on my shoulder and guided me to the table and pushed me down in a chair. She poured coffee and said, "Come on. I want to hear it."

"I don't know what he wants anymore."

Phoebe got this look on her face like the milk in her coffee was sour.

For some reason, I didn't tell her he was going to hit me, or about shoving me. I was embarrassed—for him and for me—and to tell seemed ... like I'd be showing Phoebe the two of us with all of the blemishes people want to cover up. And I didn't mention my latest problem with his age.

So I only told her about going to the festival and about him being cranky. Phoebe frowned and said, "Hmmm" a lot. Finally, she said, "Look. Something's going on with your ... Oh! I'm just going to call him Joe like you do. Something's going on with Joe and I don't know what it is. But I can tell you it isn't your fault. It is never—do you hear me?—it is *never* the fault of the kid." She left the room and came back with a large gift bag. "But there is something I can do for you right now."

A present. A present for me.

I reached through the tissue paper. The first package was a black dress, sleeveless, with a bit of a scoop neck. "Keep going. You'll see."

The second package was a pair of long black satin gloves—elbow length. I fumbled as I reached for the third package because I knew ... I hoped I knew. Out tumbled a huge pearl necklace and big earrings and a jeweled hair pin.

"Come on, Audrey. Let's get you ready for your close-up!"

I was glad I'd showered and shaved and remembered to wear my Dove deodorant. I ran to her bedroom and slipped the dress on over my head.

"Okay, now, don't look." And she turned me away from the mirror and pulled my hair up and twisted it and stuck in about two dozen bobby pins and told me to hold my breath and shut my eyes, as she glued me together with hairspray. She put the jewels on me and found a pair of shoes in her closet and smiled. "Are you ready?" She let me look in the mirror and I almost fainted.

It was her. I mean, I was her. Audrey Hepburn. I was glamorous and I actually, really and truly, almost looked like Audrey Hepburn. I have a big mouth—a horse mouth Sebastian told me. And really heavy eyebrows, but so did Audrey Hepburn in another movie called *Funny Face*. Sebastian called me a Neanderthal and scary looking. If I ever saw him again, I'd show him!

But now ... was that why I liked the poster so much? I recognized someone who looked a bit like me? With my hair pulled back and up, I could see a resemblance. I stared and stared at myself until I realized how conceited I was!

Phoebe was watching me. "So, why do you go about with that terrible mop of hair in your face? And those clothes! Do you have anything nicer than baggy this, that, and the other?"

I shook my head. "Joe hates fashion. Clothes, hair, and ... and ..." I trailed off because even to me it sounded so ridiculous. "He says it's all hypocritical?" I couldn't help the question in my voice. "He wants me to be a feminist."

(An aside: I know now how stupid that was. I mean, the older I got, the less he let me think for myself.)

"And so you can be! But there's nothing wrong with always looking your best. You needn't look like a boy who sleeps in his clothes and doesn't wash."

I cringed at what she thought of me. "Do you think ... do you think if Joe saw me like this, he might, I don't know exactly, maybe like me more? He makes me dress like a lump, but maybe he just doesn't know what I should ... could look like."

I'm sick of the sight of you.

"He'd be crazy not to be thrilled with how beautiful you are," declared Phoebe.

"Thrilled" might be a bit too much to expect. But surely he'd be just a little bit pleased?

I went back to our apartment and waited. I wasn't sure what I would do if he didn't come home until late. What if my hair didn't stay stuck?

I waited and waited and it got darker and darker. We had a curtain but I didn't pull it. Being inside this apartment with the curtain closed seemed worse than staring out at the night sky. Seemed to cut me off even more. Oh! I'm not getting this right!

I wanted to go back to Phoebe, but I thought she might be fed up with me and my problems. She'd looked so tired earlier. I turned my phone off. If she did call to ask how the new me went over, maybe she would think Joe and I went out to celebrate the new me. And I couldn't use my phone with Joe around.

He didn't come home. At midnight I gave up. I brushed out my hair and took off my dress. I put my jeans and sweatshirt on, though, not my nightgown. If he did come home, I wanted to be dressed because ...

Creepy.

Escape

In the morning, washing my face, I yanked all my hair into a ponytail and stared at myself in the mirror. I didn't know who I was anymore. I'd only found out about my mother and Joe a few weeks ago, and now there were gaping holes in the story.

I knew I didn't want to go on living like this. All these secrets. Stuff not adding up. I didn't have a friend to talk this over with, other than some grownups who might have their own problems and not a lot of patience for mine. People had always been kind, but could I depend on that much longer? What if there was only so much kindness allotted per person and I'd used up my quota?

I let out my hair and gave it a good brush and had a brainstorm. I walked to a salon I'd seen with a sign in the window that said they cut hair and donated it for wigs for women with cancer.

The woman looked a bit confused. "Are you sure, honey? Shouldn't you have your mom with you?"

"My mom died." (Truth.) "Of cancer." (Lie.) "So, I want to do this. It's my turn to be kind."

They said my hair was more than long enough so they washed it and combed it and then they snipped it off in one long braid.

"Do you want us to style it for you? We do it half-price as a thank you," the woman told me.

I nodded. "But could you cut it some more? Really short? I'm sick of it." Pause. "Sick of the sight of it."

She did what I asked and put some gel in it and spiked it up a bit. "You should always wear your hair short," she advised. "You have the bone structure." She held up a mirror and I couldn't help smiling. I looked so different!

I tried to buy a tube of the gel, but she gave me the half-empty tube she'd been using. "Sorry about your mother, dear. You've done a good thing."

More kindness from a stranger. I felt a bit guilty, but I was only trying to pay back some of the kindness shown to me. Surely a small fib was okay?

I couldn't bear to go back to the apartment. I had the idea to make minestrone soup for dinner, just like the old days, just in case Joe showed up. And I would visit Mrs. Martino on my way to Kensington Market for cheese.

She was home and thrilled to see me.

"Bella!" She hugged me so tight. "You look gorgeous! Sophia Loren! Gina Lollobrigida, for sure!" She turned me side to side. "And you're wearing the brassiere. Good. That's good." She pinched my cheeks.

I didn't tell her anything about Joe's grumpiness or our fights. (I was wearing a long-sleeve shirt to cover the bruise on my arm.)

We walked to (name withheld) cheese shop and then we had an espresso and gelato. But this time, I insisted on treating. Of course, Mrs. Martino protested.

"I have lots of money now! I do some odd jobs for a woman in my building. She gets tired and needs me." I heard the pride in my voice. I was proud to be needed by someone!

"Then I accept your generosity. Grazia, bella." She sipped her espresso. "Now, tell me. You have a boyfriend?"

I shook my head.

"Your period? Sheeza come?"

"Nope."

"Soon. You watch. Soon, for sure. You be ready."

Tears filled my eyes. We hugged again and turned away from each other and I wanted to run after her and live in her home on Sullivan Street.

The front door was unlocked. As soon as I pushed it open, I saw.

Suitcases. Mine from Mrs. Petovsky. And another one.

I saw the shock on his face when he saw my hair. He came toward me.

"What did you do?" There was an expression on his face I couldn't understand. Scared? Why?

"Cut it off." I don't know what made me go on. "I was sick of the sight of it, Joe."

He stared for a moment, a hard look coming into his eyes. "We're leaving. Get your stuff."

"What do you mean?"

"You know what I mean. We're leaving. Pack what you want. Hurry up."

He turned his back. And that did it.

"No. You tell me what's going on. You *tell* me." My voice trembled and I hated myself.

Counted the seconds. One. Two. Three.

He turned around. "Something's come up. Something

I didn't foresee. It's not safe yet, after all. Pack."

"Safe? What are you talking about? Are you in trouble?" Had he been stealing? These "friends" he mentioned. Who were they? I even thought about a gang. Was he part of something illegal? Again, I remembered the bundles of money.

"Not me. You." Suddenly he smiled. "Oh, Rebby. I'm so worried about you. About us. It's someone from the past. I heard ... well, I'll tell you everything as soon as we're safe. But right now, we've gotta get out of here. Please."

I didn't move. My heart pounded hard.

"We're on a bus tonight. A friend's driving us out of town and we'll catch the bus from there. Please hurry, Rebby. You know I only want the best for you. That's all I've always wanted. You know that."

The look on his face was sad and begging and kind, all at once, all mixed together. A loving father.

A lie. A lying father.

"I know I've been off lately. Not myself. I'm sorry. I really am. Please believe me." He put a hand to his face and wiped at his eyes. "My little Rebby," he whispered.

Once, I would have run to him. I would have been so upset with myself for upsetting him. Even the other night, on my birthday. I told him I was sorry because I just wanted to go back to things being the same. But now? I did not believe him. Didn't believe he was crying, either.

Something walked up my spine. I knew I was in trouble. I thought of Jordan's parents not wanting their daughter around him.

"Okay," I whispered. "Okay, I'll pack. Whatever you say." I made my legs move. I put the groceries on the kitchen counter. "I planned to make soup for us." I faked a smile. "I wanted to make up for misbehaving." Somehow, I managed to say those words and go to my bedroom.

He'd already been through it. The closet was empty. The mattress flipped. Stuff piled on the floor. The plain bra, my Audrey Hepburn clothes and poster. He'd found everything. Everything I'd hidden from him.

He was behind me. I could smell him. Musty. And B.O. "I'm very disappointed in you, you know. You defied me. Went against my orders."

I couldn't face him.

"But ... I guess you're growing up. I guess I have to accept a bit of back talk. Your mom was like that. Mouthy." Big sigh. "We can talk about it when we're safe again. Figure out some new rules for you."

Even now, even now, writing about this, I do not know where I got the courage.

"Thanks, Joe. You're right. I guess it's puberty. I read that. Read that girls get moody and make wrong choices."

"In that book? *Your Changing Body*? Where did you get that book, by the way?"

I lied. "At a rummage sale. I ... I wanted to understand why I was getting so silly ... so emotional. But I'll do better. I'll listen and behave."

"That's my girl. That's my little Rebby."

I picked up a garbage bag. "I'll dump all this ... junk. Then I'll pack. Just the stuff you say. Okay?"

He nodded. He watched as I threw a few other things into the bag to make it look more believable. Shook my head and rolled my eyes as if I couldn't believe how silly I'd been. An empty perfume bottle. An empty marmalade jar. Silly silly silly girl.

I walked out of my room, crossed the living room, walked down the hall. Hand on the doorknob. Turned. "What time do we leave?" Did I look eager?

"Forty-five minutes. Okay?"

"You know, I hate this place, Joe. Leaving will be great."

He closed our door, but I knew he'd watch through

the peephole. I turned right and went to the garbage chute. I opened it and pushed the bag in. Don't cry! Don't cry! It's just stuff. I could get more stuff.

I slammed the chute. Waited a second, rattled it, and slammed it again, as if I was having a problem getting the bag to fit in and go down.

I had five seconds. If he was waiting at the door for me to come back. Five seconds before he'd wonder what was taking me too long.

I ran. Ran for the stairs. If he wondered in six seconds, seven seconds, he'd go to the elevator.

Open the door. How heavy it was! Tugged it hard. Tried to push it shut. Run! Hurry! Up the stairs. Up and up. Two flights. Run! I tripped and crashed my left knee into the step. Get up! Another door. Push!

In the hallway, fumbling for the keys in my pocket. Dropped them. Grabbed at them. Missed. Clutching at air. Picked them up. Clumsy, so clumsy! In the lock. Turn. Push. Fingers on alarm. Hurry! Hurry! Close the door. Lock it. Set the alarm. Hold my breath. Listen.

Breathe.

Hiding

I spent four days at Phoebe's. From that Tuesday night to Saturday. Hardly moved. Didn't make a sound. Afraid to flush the toilets more than once a day—what if the pipes rattled? No lights. No TV.

I sat in her beautiful chairs and read. I ate what she'd left in the fridge. What I found in the cupboards. Rationed it out. No cooking. No smells. And when it got dark, I opened the curtain and watched the sky until I fell asleep.

I pretended I was Phoebe. I pretended this apartment was mine and, just like Phoebe, I was a recluse. I pretended I was famous and, if I went outside, I'd be spotted and chased by adoring fans and paparazzi. "I want to be alone," I said out loud.

Except I didn't. I didn't want to be alone anymore. And *never* alone with Joe.

Twice that week I had that ... weird feeling. A memory or

sensation. Awake and dreaming. Scared. I wanted Mommy.

I took my clothes off on Thursday and looked at myself in the full-length mirror. Never had a full-length mirror before. Saw the cut on my knee and the bruise on my shin. Saw the bruise on my arm. And I saw that I—my body—was starting to change. Like Mrs. Wasserman's book promised. And I wondered what it must be like to have scars where ... where Phoebe had them.

I sponged in the sink, afraid to let the water run loud in the tub.

Did I have a plan? I'm trying to remember. No. Of course I didn't. I couldn't think past the minute—the moment—I was in. Except when I read. Phoebe had so many books. When I read, time passed. When I read, I forgot about myself. I wanted to be like the women in Phoebe's books, books Joe would never have let me read. I wanted their courage. And when I finished those books and came back to myself, I was shocked to remember. Shocked I'd forgotten.

On Saturday night, I heard the key in the lock and, for a moment, was terrified. I wanted to hide but I couldn't move as I watched the door open and Phoebe was home.

She wasn't surprised to see me. And then she was. She

looked me up and down and stared at my face. "What is it? Rebecca? What's wrong?"

I couldn't figure out where to begin.

"You look awful. And you're wearing one of my wigs."

I grabbed at it. Yanked it from my head. Stared at the long blonde curls.

"Rebecca?" She put down her bag and came toward me. She was smiling. Worried. Not mad. "You've cut your hair."

I started shaking.

"Sweetheart? Please tell me." She took my hand.

"I ran away," I blurted. "He ... he said we had to leave. Again. He hurt me. He hit me and pinched me and pushed me. And, oh, Phoebe, he said I was a bitch and ungrateful. But he's lying. I know it. It's all lies. All of it. I'm sure of it. My whole life. Lies. But I don't know what the lies are!"

Phoebe held me tight and said, "Shhh, shhh ..." over and over. She pulled me down on the couch and gave me tissues and said, "Keep going."

And so I did. Right up to running to her apartment. "I never told him. Never. About you. About having a key. So, I came here. Please don't be mad at me."

"Oh, for the love of ..." She finally took off her coat. "I'm ordering a pizza and you're going to flush the toilets and take a shower. Then we'll figure out what's going on. I'll get you a pair of my pajamas, and I'm burning your clothes."

I tidied up in the bathroom and washed and the pizza came and her first question was, "Why the wig?"

"A disguise?" I asked. "If I had to leave here, maybe he ... no one would notice me straightaway." I didn't tell her I was pretending to be her.

We talked more, but I was yawning and she made me go to her guest room, and I woke up the next day at noon. For a moment, I didn't know where I was, and when I remembered, I was scared. But then I really remembered, and the hard knot in my stomach went away and I went to find Phoebe.

She was in the kitchen with Doug.

"How are you, Rebecca? Phoebe tells me you've been through a lot."

I could smell alcohol, but he wasn't slurring his words. I guess I looked stupid. About Doug, I mean, because he laughed. "I know I smell, but I splash it on. Even the piss. Every day before my shift. And I don't brush my teeth, either. Wife doesn't like it."

"So you're not ... um ..."

"Nope. Still gainfully employed, Rebecca. On the job every day."

"Doug's been a friend of mine for years," Phoebe explained. "I asked him to help us out." She handed me a mug of coffee and pointed to a slice of peanut butter toast. "By the way, he's gone. Joe's gone. The super saw him leave last Tuesday night with a suitcase. He hasn't picked up any of the junk mail in your slot. No sign of him. Doug wants us to go to the apartment. He needs to take a look around."

I stiffened.

"We'll be with you," Doug said.

Nothing made sense. It was like they had watched the whole TV show and I was starting in the middle of season two. But I went downstairs with them and into the apartment. And ... I know it was silly of me, but I felt embarrassed for Phoebe to see how ugly this apartment was. To know where—how—I'd been living.

The suitcase was where I'd left it. My bedroom was trashed—worse than before. He'd found my Audrey Hepburn jewels. They were ground to bits on the floor. Phoebe and Doug shook their heads, and I caught them giving each other looks. Like they knew something I didn't.

"He did this? Not you?"

"When he realized ... realized I got away, he must have come back and done this." Then I saw the phone charger. He had pulled it out of the plug and thrown it on the mattress. So he knew. I imagined his face when he found it. I picked it up.

"I didn't have this when I ran. Just my phone. But if he saw this ... I mean, he *did* see this. So, he'd know I had a phone and he wouldn't know how or ... or ..." I looked at them. "He'd be furious. He'd be so ..." I couldn't finish. And I was shaking again.

"Let's get out of here." Phoebe put her arm around me.

Doug went through all the garbage pails. Then, back upstairs, he asked me questions. About where we lived before. Streets and towns. Any detail I could remember. He said he would talk to people at the places where I'd lived. See if he could put some facts together. Figure out where Joe might have gone.

Questions. So many questions. I knew I had to do it— keep answering questions. I knew that. I felt like a traitor. I couldn't get it through my head what Joe had done. But what had he done, exactly?

And so they asked more questions, and some questions twice.

"Tell us how he hurt you."

So I did. But I still felt like I shouldn't. "Maybe it was my fault?"

I saw Phoebe and Doug glance at each other. And then the awful question from Doug. "Rebecca. Did he ever ... touch you ... in an inappropriate way?"

"I don't know what you mean."

"Straight up, then," Phoebe said. "Sexual abuse. Did he put his hands ..."

"No!" I shouted.

Phoebe hugged me. "We're sorry. We are. But the police must know everything."

"Why?" My voice rose in a wail.

"We want to find him, Rebecca," Doug said.

I don't, I thought.

By the end of the day, all Doug had found was nothing. No trace of Joe Greene or Rebecca Greene. If Rebecca Greene was born on September 26th, 1992, there wasn't a record of it.

Lost

The next day, Doug came back and said we were going to the police station.

"Why? Why do we have to go to the police station?"

From the way he and Phoebe looked at me I could tell they knew something and wouldn't tell.

My stomach cramped when we got to the front door of the apartment building. I hadn't been outside in over a week, and I didn't want to go outside now.

"What a glorious sunny day," said Phoebe. She gave me a pair of her sunglasses. "Put them on, darling. You can do this."

I remembered the first day I saw her—wearing sunglasses in the rain—and fell in love with her. I put on the sunglasses and went through the door.

There was a police car in front, and an officer held the door. And I realized that if Joe was watching ...

"He isn't here." But I saw Phoebe look around as she hustled me into the back seat.

At the station, Doug said, "Rebecca, this is Grace. She's a detective with the Missing Persons Bureau."

Grace smiled at me. "How are you doing?"

I wiped sweaty hands on my jeans. "Missing Persons? So you've found Joe?" I looked past her, expecting to see him answering questions on the other side of the glass wall. I clenched my jaw to not throw up.

"Not exactly," Grace answered, her eyes on mine. "We've found you."

Phoebe put her arm around me and pulled me to sit down beside her.

"We think we know why Joe fled," Doug said. He handed me a piece of paper. My hand was shaking and Phoebe held me tighter. "This was posted a couple of weeks ago by Missing Persons. We're going on the assumption that Joe saw it."

It was a flyer about a missing child, abducted in 1994. Victoria Emily Kennedy. Last seen at her daycare in Toronto. Three years old. Born May 24, 1991. Believed to be in British Columbia. They had aged the photo to what she might look like today.

She was a teenager. She had very dark hair and a wide mouth and heavy eyebrows. Blue eyes.

I stared at this picture—this picture that was me and couldn't be me. It was like looking in a mirror. A slightly warped mirror. "This isn't me?"

Phoebe nodded yes. "It is you. It is."

I couldn't get my mouth to work, couldn't get any saliva in my mouth. "I'm ..." I swallowed. "A missing person? Me?"

Phoebe and Joe and Grace watched me.

"But how ...? I mean ..." I shook my head, trying to unscramble my thinking. "Where did you get this? I mean, who is left to do this? Look for me? No one is looking for me. Everyone is dead."

And Found

Phoebe figured out my problem before the others. She knew that my mother died in childbirth. My fault.

"Oh, darling!" She put her hands on my face. "She's not dead. Your mother isn't dead. You have a family. Grandparents and ... they've been searching for you."

Stunned. Like in Peking Garden. My life turned upside down and inside out. Again.

This is what they told me:

- My mother's name is Gloria.
- She was eighteen when she met John Miller.
- John Miller—Joe—is ten years older than Gloria.
- Her parents didn't like how John ordered Gloria around. They suspected he hit Gloria but she wouldn't tell.
- She broke up with him and he threatened her.

- He never knew she was pregnant.
- When I was three, I was abducted from my daycare.
- A family—grandparents, aunts, uncles, cousins, a half-brother—is waiting to meet me.
- My name is Victoria and I am thirteen years old.

Going Home

The next morning, Phoebe helped me pack a carry-on suitcase. She gave me some of her clothes because mine were shabby and I was embarrassed. I didn't need much, of course. I figured I was just staying overnight, maybe two nights, and then back here.

"How are you, darling?"

"Nervous!" My thoughts were a big jumble. Would they like me? Wish I wasn't found? Probably they'd think me weird or ... well, since I'd never gone to school, would they think I was stupid? At least my jeans were new, and Phoebe gave me a sweater that was supposed to look big, so I didn't look too awful. I scrubbed myself really hard in the shower and brushed my teeth twice, and remembered to use deodorant and Q-tips (because of my short hair, earwax shows). And what would I say? Should I bring some of my book reports to prove I can read and write?

"And mad. Really mad. I'm a teenager! I've been a teenager for almost a year and a half, and I didn't know. He took *that* from me, too."

Phoebe came with me. We went with Grace and we drove the Gardiner Expressway and along Lakeshore and back up to Queen Street in the east end. I thought it was eerie to see the 501 streetcar coming toward me, heading west, from where I had just come—my past and present tied together. Twenty-nine minutes apart. We parked in front of 258 Glenbay Road.

I got out of the car, leaning into Phoebe, my knees not working properly. I gazed at the house, hoping for memories. A two-storied house with an attic. I stared at that attic window and knew the truth of another lie.

Phoebe tugged me forward. "Come on, darling," she whispered in my ear. "This is your big close-up."

She got me to smile, even as my eyes got watery. *I can do this. I can do this.* And I made myself move to the steps leading off the sidewalk.

At the bottom step, in the cement, two small footprints.

And on the verandah, a woman with black hair.

She opened her arms wide, but crumpled to her knees, and her head fell back and her mouth opened, but no sound came out. An older woman came through the door and touched her on the shoulder and moved down the steps to me.

"Oh, honey. Oh, sweetheart. Vicky. My little Vicky. Look at you! Look at you!"

In a second, the woman with black hair was in the middle of us, holding my face in her hands, searching my eyes. My mother. My mother who looked like Audrey Hepburn. And I remembered how Joe looked scared when he saw that poster. Now I knew why.

"I never stopped. Oh, my sweetheart. Never. Never thought ... never allowed myself to think ..."

"Bunrab."

"Bunrab?"

"Bunrab. My bunny rabbit."

"Yes. Yes! You remember?"

I nodded and wiped my nose as a little boy squirmed in beside me and held out a drawing.

"I drewed it for you."

It was a picture of a girl with black hair, except the girl was split in a funny way down the middle. She had a head, but only half a body. A right arm and a left leg.

"It's you. See?" He pointed. "A half a sister. They said I

have a half a sister now." He smiled, pleased with himself. "I'm Cody and I'm free." He held up three fingers. "Grandma made a cake and I helped, and I think we should eat it."

Somebody laughed and somebody else, until everyone was laughing, including me, and I felt like a balloon with all the air out. The older woman put her arm under mine and around my body and we went inside.

We sat around the dining room table, and everyone told me who they were and tried to fill in ten missing years. I met my grandparents, of course, and Aaron, too. He and Gloria got married five years ago and had Cody.

"And we live here with my parents because ..."

"Because after you disappeared," my grandfather continued, "we became a different kind of family. Stuck together. Right, Aaron?"

Aaron smiled. "Yes, sir. Great house. Free babysitting. What's not to love?" He turned to me. "I do contract work for the Ontario government and travel a lot. I like to think of Gloria here with Cody. Safer."

"Safer?" And then I understood. Of course. Of course. Why wouldn't Joe come back? Why wouldn't he keep hurting this family? And now? With me gone? Would he try something else?

"*Very* safe," my grandmother answered.

"Don't you worry," Phoebe said to me. "Offsir Doug's on it."

I laughed and told them about Doug. "And he actually splashes himself every day with alcohol and piss!" When they all stared at me, I slapped my hand over my mouth. "Sorry. But that's what he said."

There were questions and answers and stories told and photos to look at. I do remember one funny thing. This woman who is my grandmother asked if I wanted milk or juice with my cake, and I said I'd like coffee. They all seemed a bit surprised by this, and that's when Phoebe decided to explain things about my life that I didn't know needed any explaining. Apparently, it isn't normal (that word again) for twelve—I mean thirteen-year-olds to drink coffee.

"And shall I call you Gloria?" I asked my mother. "I called him Joe, so I wondered."

The man who was my grandfather dropped his fork. My mother put out her hand to his.

"No. No, Vicky. I want you to call me Mother. Or Mom. I've waited ten years for you ... to hear you say Mother."

Before I could answer, Cody said, "Or Mommy. I says Mommy." He winked at me and I felt my heart squeeze.

And what was my name? Could I really go back to Victoria?

My grandmother said, "We never called you that. Always Vicky."

"I named you Victoria because you were born on May 24th. Queen Victoria's birthday," explained my mother. "But you were such a tiny little thing, just over six pounds, that Victoria seemed too grand for you."

"Tiny? But he told me I was a big baby. He said I was so big, that's why you died. He said it was my fault."

Everyone gasped and my grandfather swore. Phoebe came up behind me and put her hands on my shoulders. "And yet she is the most *delightful* child that I have ever met." I didn't understand what she meant, and when I turned to look at her, she was almost glaring at the others, as if daring them to contradict her.

Gloria ... my mother ... got up and said, "Come with me." She held out her hand and I clutched it.

She walked me around the house, and I'd catch a glimpse of a memory before it disappeared. "Oh, wasn't that ..." I'd trail off because whatever I started to say wasn't there anymore. As if memories liked playing hide and seek.

"This is where you took your first step," my mother

pointed. "Right here between the kitchen table and the sink. And this is where you fell on the step and cut your lip. And see here? Here are the marks we made on the wall as you got bigger."

I looked at the scratches. There were three. And then there were none.

She took me upstairs and into a small bedroom. The walls were soft yellow—egg yolks beaten with sugar. There were ivory lace curtains and a bedspread covered in spring flowers—yellow daffodils, pink tulips, sprays of mauve lilac, lily of the valley—all soft and running together like an Impressionist painting. There was a dresser with photos—*photos!*—me and my mom and my grandparents. A bookshelf, and on top was a raggedy bunny rabbit.

"This was my room. This was my room."

"It is your room." My grandfather stood in the doorway.

"It ..." And for some reason this hadn't occurred to me. I didn't know, hadn't thought that ... I'd live here? I figured I'd stay with Phoebe, maybe, or ... Or what? Honestly, sometimes I'm so stupid I can't believe it!

"Do you ... Will I ..." I couldn't look at them. I stared at the floor.

Gloria ... my mother ... sat on the bed and pulled me onto her lap, just as if I was a little girl. "We do and you will. Understand? Look at me. We *do* want you and you *will* live here." She kissed the top of my head.

"And that's the end of that nonsense," said my grandfather.

Adjusting

On Thanksgiving, I insisted on making minestrone soup. I said it was auspiciously appropriate for me to give thanks. (An aside: They seemed surprised I could cook, but they seemed pleasantly surprised that I could eat with a knife and fork. They obviously were worried I had led a very ~~daralick~~ derelict life.)

And they laughed at the big words I used. Like "auspiciously" and "derelict."

Nor would they let me go out on my own at all. They insisted on taking me to the store for ingredients for the soup. "I'm used to taking the subway and streetcars," I said. "You don't have to worry about me."

But of course they did worry, and sometimes I felt like a prisoner.

I asked to invite Mr. and Mrs. Martino for Thanksgiving and they came with a tiramisu for dessert. They had wonderful stories about me and had a lot to say about Joe.

My grandmother said, "I am so grateful that Vicky had guardian angels looking over her."

"And Mrs. Martino even bought me a bra! Joe wouldn't let me have a bra because he said ..." I stopped. I didn't want to talk about *him* at Thanksgiving. And I was confused by the look on my mother's face. "Are you mad at me?"

"At you? How could I possibly be mad at you?"

Without thinking, I said, "Bastardo!" Spit, spit. (Pretend spit.)

Again, all the funny looks! Mrs. Martino jumped in to explain.

The next week, and for the first time, I went to a doctor and got a full check-up and vaccinations. I went to a dentist and ended up with braces. I got a library card!

Weeks later, the police arrested Joe in Saskatchewan. Nothing to do with me. He was caught robbing houses. But then the computer cross-referenced (that's what Aaron told me) with other police forces and found out about the abduction, and he didn't get out on bail. (An aside: it seems fitting, doesn't it, that a computer program caught him?)

I don't know yet if I'll have to see him again or go to court or, well, anything.

My mother said she was excited about that. "Don't you worry. If that piece of ... poop thinks I'd be too scared to face him, he's in for a rude awakening. In fact, I hope I do get to see him in handcuffs!"

I thought about that. I imagined the scene. Me and Mom, arms around each other. We wouldn't have to say anything. Just smile the bad smile and look at him.

Finally, I was allowed to leave the house alone! And so, at long last, I found myself sitting at a desk in a Grade 7 classroom. I should have been in Grade 8, but they wanted to see if I could cope. I could cope with the work. Coping with sitting still was tedious.

I am in therapy. The first therapist was awful. She wanted me to talk about how damaged I was feeling. I didn't feel damaged and said so, and she said I was too damaged to know any better. I refused to talk to her anymore.

The second therapist is much more understanding. Or at least she lets me talk and doesn't tell me what I'm feeling.

And what I am feeling is this: a Picasso painting—looking at my life from all angles at once and trying to make sense of it. Shape it into something that looks like a human being.

Sometimes, something knots in my tummy and

pushes up through my chest and I think I am suffocating. Until it comes out—a garbled scream or tears. Everything a lie. And all done out of spite and revenge and control. Not love.

Sometimes, I haven't thought about him and I suddenly remember, and it is as if I just lost my footing and stumbled. One day, I put on my grandmother's reading glasses and it was like that. Things did not line up properly.

And then the nightmare started.

I hear the door open and I can't move. He stands there, watching. *Come with me, Rebby. The bus is leaving. You belong to me.*

I jerk to sitting and he is gone.

When I shook off the nightmare, I slipped from the bed to the window. A deep breath and I peeked around the curtain. A streetlight shone clear on the lawn and sidewalk and parked cars. A shadow moved across the street. Someone was bending down behind a car. My body clenched. And then a man stood up, tugging on a leash, and I saw the Golden Retriever from three doors away.

The next night he walks to the dresser. I watch him pick up the photo of my mother and me. *Put it down!* I scream at him. He tosses it from one hand to the other, once pretending to drop it. *Oops!* He smiles the bad smile. *They don't want you here, Rebby. They want Cody. Not you. Do the right thing and leave. You belong to me.*

I gasp and wake up.

He wasn't really here. I knew that. But he *had* been in this house, years ago. He knew his way around this house.

I tiptoed downstairs and wandered around the house in the dark, trying not to bump into anything. I invented a game. If I could remember where everything was in the dark and not bump into things, then it meant this was my home. My forever home. Like with rescue dogs.

I got back into bed with my book, *Harry Potter and the Prisoner of Azkaban.* I knew I wouldn't fall asleep.

The next night I hear a tapping at my window. And I get up and look out and he is there. On a ladder like the handyman one. *I can't come in anymore. That therapist you're blabbing to won't let me in. You have to come out. Run away. Before you grow up.*

I went downstairs and walked through the living room and hit so many things in the dark with my toe, my shin, my hand. *I don't belong. I don't belong here.* I sat down, shaking.

"There is nothing to fear," my grandparents told me. All the locks were changed when it happened. And changed to better locks after they found me. There were bars on the basement windows, too. But I saw a bit of light under the kitchen door. And I heard something, some little rustling noise. I don't know how I had the courage to walk across the living room and put my hand on the door. But I did. I pushed it, and it swung wide open.

My grandfather, wearing his old navy robe my mother makes fun of, was eating a butterscotch pudding cup.

"You caught me," he said. "You won't tell on me, will you?" (An aside: This is funny, kind of, because my grandfather is a retired high school principal. Maybe I should get him and Mr. Popolopolos together?)

I shook my head. "I won't tell."

"Then I'll give you my last one. I hide them at the back of the cupboard. Your grandmother fusses about my diabetes." He handed me the cup and a spoon. "Couldn't sleep?" He put his hand over mine, and I stared at the sunspots and veins, and when I cried, he wiped my face with the back of that hand.

"Bad dream?"

I nodded. "He used to ... sometimes ... come into my

room at night. He'd take something of mine and ... and I'd find it later. Torn up. Broken."

"That's what his kind does. Tears up families. Breaks hearts. Doesn't care. Just about hurting folks. Just about power."

"I keep dreaming he comes into my bedroom. Even now. Even though I know he's in prison."

"He can never hurt you again, my dear."

I nodded.

"So take a deep breath and let it out. Like Dr. Roberta told you." He squeezed my hand.

Breath in. Breath out.

I looked around the kitchen. At the yellow ducks on the wallpaper, at Cody's drawing of me on the fridge. Last week he filled in the other half. It was lopsided, and that seemed appropriate. My grandfather was watching me, his blue eyes full of worry.

I smiled at him and peeled back the tinfoil on my pudding cup. "I bet they don't have butterscotch pudding cups in prison," I said.

"I bet you're right."

The next day my grandmother found my birthday sweater in the Goodwill collection bag, and she poked at the loose bit of wool. "I can knit this up for you, if you'd like. Good as new."

I thought about it. I'd bought the sweater for myself, after all. It had nothing to do with him. But now, when I looked at it, all I could think about was the bus ride home on my fake birthday. I shook my head.

Some things should remain unraveled.

Victoria

Near Christmas, I went to Phoebe's overnight.

I rode the streetcar along Queen, from one end to the other, sitting in the seat by the driver so I could see all the lights coming toward me. From my new home, past my old neighborhood of Sullivan Street, and on and along to the bleak and dreary apartment building and Phoebe's home in Parkdale.

It occurred to me that Queen Street was like a river, flowing through the city, depositing me here and there along its banks. And the street and I were named for the same woman, Queen Victoria. And finally, finally, one huge problem was solved. For weeks I waffled between Rebecca and Vicky. I didn't want to be Rebecca anymore. I didn't want anything he gave me! But sometimes I didn't answer when they called me Vicky at home or at school. I didn't realize they were talking to me. And now I had an idea. No one called her Queen Vicky, I bet. So, I would be Victoria. No more nicknames for me!

I got off and ran across the street and, for one awful moment, I remembered and I felt sick. And I couldn't help it—I looked around as if I'd see him watching me. So, I did what Dr. Roberta told me to do. "Don't try to deny it," she said. "When it comes, let the feeling be there. Don't push it away. Take a really good close look at it. And breathe."

I am feeling afraid.

Breath in and breath out.

I imagine him leaning against the entrance, smiling the bad smile.

Breath in and breath out.

I imagine looking at him, looking him right in the eye.

Breath in and breath out.

Liar.

Breath in and breath out.

I think of my grandfather.

Fear leaves with the breath.

For now.

I pressed the buzzer. "It's Victoria!"

Phoebe looked a bit tired. Maybe because she had gone to the trouble of getting a whole meal ready. I was glad it was something hearty like lasagna, because she looked thinner, too.

"I'm dying to hear everything. I've been so bored since you left. Just ho-hum around here now, dahlink!"

"Well ... did you see my interview in *The Star*? Gloria had allowed one interview because they kept calling after he went to jail." (An aside: I finally got my wish and got my picture in the newspaper, and boy, I sure became famous! People who'd met me over the years sent cards, and Mrs. Tokiwa mailed me that silk scarf. And Jordan's whole family came to meet my family.)

"Of course I saw it! Bought three copies. What else have you been up to?"

I told her about school. "And Jordan and I are friends again. And ... I sort of have a boyfriend."

"You do? Who? Come on. Tell me everything!" Phoebe demanded.

"It's Sebastian. The one who called me a Neanderthal and a hairy ape. But he's matured."

For some reason, Phoebe laughed. "What's he like?"

"Cute. I didn't notice before. And he's really smart. He helped me figure out computers." And I thought about him squashing in beside me at a desk chair and our legs touching, and him leaning over me to show me how to cut and paste, and how I could smell his toothpaste and the gel in his hair, and even the laundry detergent his mom used. (Sunlight.) And he put his hand over mine on the mouse and then he turned to say something and I turned to listen and our mouths were so close, and so he bobbed his head and his lips touched mine and I thought I was going to fall off my chair.

"He says he's always liked me. He's even stopped calling me names."

I told her about Dr. Roberta. "I like her. She never tries to tell me how I'm feeling. Not like some people. Some people say I'm in denial. What does that even mean? I'm not denying anything. They say I'm too happy. But what do they know? They don't see me when I'm all alone. They don't see me staring at all the photos of everyone, wishing I was in them."

"Oh, cripes!" Phoebe rolled her eyes. "According to 'some people' (and she made air quotes around the words), I should be dead, or at least penniless. That's one reason I changed my name and hid out."

"One day Dr. Roberta asked a funny question. She wanted to know if I felt like I'd lost ten years."

"And?"

"I didn't lose them! Not like money fell out of my pocket. Not like I was in a coma and woke up and said, 'Where am I?' So how can my life be lost? I mean, who was living my life for ten years if not me?"

Phoebe smiled. "Sounds like you're teaching Dr. Roberta a thing or two!"

"And then she asked if I felt like I'd missed out on belonging to my family."

"And you said?"

"I said yes. But I didn't know it then. I only know it *now. Then* I didn't feel I didn't belong. I had a dad and neighbors and some friends, and you." I cleared the dishes and served up candy-cane ice cream. "It's very confusing. But Sebastian told me about Picasso, so I think my life is like that. I mean ... what I mean to say is, he drew people from all angles—like one of those three-sixty mirrors. And I'm looking at my life from all angles and trying to fit them into being me."

"I'm dying to meet this Sebastian. He sounds perfect for you."

I felt my face go hot. "And what does closure mean? People say I have to have it. Or get it. But I can't figure out what it means."

"Hateful word. It means we can close off a chapter of our lives and be done with it. Never think about it again." She made a brushing motion with her hands.

I mulled this over. "Well, *that's* never going to happen! I can't stop myself from remembering things. One night, I remembered the time he said I wasn't as pretty as my mother and I'd never get a boyfriend. Well, Sebastian says I'm pretty. So there."

Phoebe said, "Why don't you write it all down? Whatever you remember. Maybe it'll be a book or a movie one day."

"Oh! Do you think so? But can I put you in it, even though you're a recluse?"

Phoebe didn't say anything, and I thought maybe I'd gone too far. But then, "Actually, I've been thinking about writing a tell-all memoir."

"Really?"

She sighed. "It's now or never. So, thank you very much, Victoria. Whatever would I have done without you?"

Which seemed an odd thing to say, if you ask me. Because, really, wasn't it the other way around?

We went to bed and I dreamed about him. He tapped on the window and I knew it was silly. We were on the penthouse floor, after all.

Last chance, Rebby. Join me now or I'll make you sorry.

I opened the window and shoved the ladder. He went sailing through the air, somersaulting over rooftops, smaller and smaller, and he was gone. I got back into bed and slept until Phoebe woke me up.

After breakfast, we went shopping on Roncesvalles and Phoebe gave me money to buy gifts for Gloria and Aaron and Cody and my grandparents.

"One day I'll pay you back," I told her.

"Oh, poo! Ever since I met you, I've been in the middle of a real live adventure as well. Best Supporting Actress. And worth every dollar."

My mother came to get me at Phoebe's. She'd been to visit before, because she said she had to know where I'd been living, where "it" happened.

"Such a beautiful apartment," she said. "I really mean it." My mother is an interior decorator, and she wouldn't lie. "And I've said this before, but I can't thank you enough. I'm ... we're all so grateful that Vicky found people like you and the Martinos and the Wassermans and ..." My mother got weepy, again, and Phoebe put her arm around her.

"I know. But please stop thanking me. Victoria has been a godsend!"

I didn't know what this meant, but it sounded nice.

The two of them hugged tightly. "Let us know your schedule," my mother said, her voice low, "and we'll be there for you. Please know that. Errands, chauffeuring, meals delivered. Whatever you need."

Phoebe suddenly looked tired again. "You got it," she whispered.

I wanted to know what they were talking about. Except the way they looked into each other's eyes made me think that this was something I shouldn't ask about. For now.

Mom and I got on the streetcar and rumbled back along Queen. So many people out in the late afternoon, shopping still, hurrying to shows or restaurants, carolers singing, children glued to store windows, skaters at City Hall, worshippers heading into churches.

Strangers. I knew that. But still I felt certain of finding kindness wherever, whenever I needed it. My eyes got teary and the rigid forms mingled, blurring and blending in the light. I leaned into my mother, my head on her shoulder.

In a few minutes, we were in the streetcar loop at the end of Queen Street, where Aaron and Cody were waiting. We joined hands and walked up the hill and home.

Mrs. Martino's Minestrone Soup

Everyone has their own recipe for this soup. Or you make it once from a recipe and then change it up. More garlic. Less broth. Swiss chard instead of kale. It doesn't matter.

Put some olive oil in a large pot.

Add in one cup each of chopped onion, chopped carrot, chopped celery. Stir and cook on medium heat until softened. Maybe ten minutes?

Add in a chopped fennel bulb and two or three chopped zucchini—green and yellow. Cook for a few more minutes.

Add in lots of chopped garlic—maybe five cloves? Buy fresh heads of garlic, not the cloves already peeled. Cook for a minute.

Add in lots of fennel seeds. One recipe says a ½-teaspoon but that's ridiculous. I like the flavor and so put in a heaping tablespoon.

You can add chili peppers now if you want. A teaspoon if you like spicy.

Add in a can of whole tomatoes and juice. Add in four cups of stock—chicken or vegetable. Mrs. Martino makes her own stock, but I buy it from a store.

Add in two cans of white kidney beans. Rinse them first.

*Secret Ingredient! Add in a good size chunk of rind off a piece of Parmigiano Reggiano cheese. Push it down in the broth.

Bring all this to a boil and cook for about 10 minutes.

Add in lots of chopped kale. Stir it all up.

Cover and simmer for an hour. Or you can make it in the morning and let it sit all day. Stir every now and then.

Mrs. Martino puts a thick slice of day-old Italian bread in each bowl and puts a bit of olive oil on the bread. Then she ladles out the soup. She sprinkles grated Parmigiano Reggiano on top.

Mrs. Martino says she hides the cooked and gooey rind and eats it herself when no one is looking.

Mrs. Martino says, if more people show up, you add another tin of beans and some more stock.

Mrs. Martino says her motto is, there is always enough.

Acknowledgments

So many thanks to my agent Barbara Berson, who took me on because of *Unravel*. She is always there with good advice, and supports me when I'm feeling bleak and dreary.

After all these years of being published, I am grateful to finally be working with my good buddy Peter Carver. We've traded war stories back and forth about this business, and now I'm proud to be one of his authors.

Thanks to Richard Dionne for publishing this book, and to Penny Hozy who offered such a competent copy edit.

I don't know how I'd get by if it weren't for my colleagues at CANSCAIP (The Canadian Society of Children's Authors, Illustrators, and Performers). They are a lovely mix of friend, cheerleader, therapist, and drinking companion.

An author needs all the "home" support she can get, and I bless my husband, kids, and friends for their encouragement and faith. I particularly want to acknowledge my wonderful Italian (in-law) family who inspired parts of this story.

And I can't forget our dogs. So many good ideas show up when walking a dog.

Photo credit: Deb Olii

Interview with Sharon Jennings

Why did you want to tell this story?

Unravel didn't begin as a story that I "wanted to tell"! I was at an outdoor literary festival and saw a photographer taking photos of kids listening to authors. I wondered what would happen if a parent didn't want their child photographed, and then I wondered about the reasons why. Within a day, I had written my first chapter. Then my characters began to take shape: Joe, a misogynist, had kidnapped his daughter and had been lying for years; Rebecca became a well-read and curious young girl who was bound to figure things out.

Although Rebecca was abducted by Joe and deceived by him for years, she never seems like a victim, but rather a girl with a lot of strength. Why was that important to you?

This is the story that I "wanted to tell"—about a strong,

intelligent young girl who could stand up to life. She is curious and insightful, generous and friendly, wise beyond her years. And because I made sure that she loved books and reading, and made friends wherever she went, I felt it made sense that she was never a victim. She had so many strong characters in books to guide her along, and so many people who took an interest in her. I've always believed that children who read have an advantage—a hidden super power—no matter what life throws at them.

As you say, Rebecca is a reader and gains a lot of comfort and knowledge from the books she consumes, despite Joe's trying to limit her access to them. Why did you want to emphasize that part of her life?

Joe wants to limit her access to books that might teach her things he doesn't want her to know—books about puberty and sex, for example. That's because he wants to keep her a little girl that he can control. He lost control of Rebecca's mother, and is still resentful. We see in many places in *Unravel* that Joe thinks women should obey their husbands and do what they're told.

What do you think it is about Rebecca that attracts Phoebe's interest from the outset?

I've modeled Rebecca, a little bit, on two young girls that I met years ago. They both had wild hair and oversized clothes, and they both were startlingly intelligent, with a quick brightness about them that attracted me. I think that Phoebe saw Rebecca, at first, as the foundling in literature that is left by fairies on the doorstep; then she discovers that Rebecca is both intelligent and innocent and she is charmed.

During her time living on Sullivan street, Rebecca finds Sebastian to be a boy who teases her, says unkind things about her, does not really display any regard for her. How do you explain that behavior, in light of his becoming a candidate to be her boyfriend in the end?

I modeled Sebastian on so many of the boys that I had crushes on in grade school! At that age, we expressed our attraction to each other by name-calling, pushing and shoving, relentless teasing, professing our disdain for the other. Sebastian and Rebecca are both intelligent, enjoy the same hobbies and interests, and it felt quite natural to me that they would make up and get together by the end of *Unravel*. I had a soft spot for Sebastian as I wrote, and wanted to give him a chance to "mature," as Victoria put it.

It turns out that Rebecca/Victoria has been separated from her mother and grandparents for ten years. And when she finally is reunited with them, she still has nightmares about being taken away from them again. How do you think an experience like this affects a young person's long term mental health?

Although I did some research about abductions, I must confess that I didn't research much about how an abducted child felt upon the discovery. I knew that might shape my story in a way that didn't fit Victoria's personality.

I wanted Victoria to comprehend what had happened to her through the filter of her very strong and mature nature. I couldn't have this incredible young woman fall apart and be unable to function. And so I decided that her fears and terrors and questions would manifest themselves in the darkness of nightmares. Of course, Victoria will always have moments or days when she is thrown off-balance, or when emotions overwhelm her. But a book has to end at some point, and I couldn't leave my readers with a sense that Victoria was falling apart.

I never know where inspiration comes from, but one of my favorite scenes in the book is Victoria and her grandfather eating pudding cups in the kitchen. It is so matter-of-fact and ordinary, and yet it says much about the comfort and love that will embrace and support Victoria going forward.

While much of this story comes out of your imagination, it also comes from your knowledge that such things do happen in the real world. How much research do you carry out when you're working on a story like this?

I read a lot about children who are abducted and what steps are taken by their families and the authorities. Every now and then I came across a good news story about a child, now a teen or an adult, who was reunited with their real family. A funny thing: so often the discovery came about by a fluke. I read one story (and I can't remember the exact details) about a boy who came across a missing person's page. He didn't know that, he was reading about himself, except that he saw a photograph in the background that was the same photograph his "mom" had. He went to the police station on his own and found out the truth. This is one reason why Joe kept Rebecca away from computers!

Phoebe is the one in the novel who encourages Victoria to write her story. What advice would you have for young writers who wish to tell stories that arise out of difficult things that actually happen to them or people they know?

As an author who visits schools often, I always encourage students to write their own stories, and not to avoid the difficult or the sad or the embarrassing moments. I tell them how many of my stories came from my life, and that I use *everything* as "grist for the mill" of writing. In Grade 5 I peed my pants running home from school, and that is now page one of my middle-grade novel *Home Free*. Recently, I began writing a memoir about growing up, and this exercise has allowed me to understand so much that was hidden from me.

Writing helps us make sense of our world and who we are in it. Writing lets us see patterns and gives us answers. Phoebe encourages Victoria to write her story in order to be in command of what happened to her. And we know that Phoebe takes her own advice and begins to write a "tell-all" memoir!

Thank you, Sharon, for your insights and your honesty.